Friedrich Max Müller

Nyaya and Vaiseshika

NYAYA AND VAISESHIKA

BY
FRIEDRICH MAX MÜLLER

SUSIL GUPTA (INDIA) LTD

INDIAN PHILOSOPHY.

BY

F. MAX MULLER

VOLUME ONE

THE SIX SYSTEMS

VOLUME TWO

VEDANTA AND PURVA-MIMAMSA

VOLUME THREE

SAMKHYA AND YOGA

VOLUME FOUR

NYAYA AND VAISESHIKA

Friedrich Max Müller

Nyaya and Vaiseshika

ISBN/EAN: 9783337384760

Printed in Europe, USA, Canada, Australia, Japan

Cover: Foto ©Andreas Hilbeck / pixelio.de

More available books at **www.hansebooks.com**

Originally published under the title of
The Six Systems of Indian Philosophy.

FIRST EDITION 1899
NEW EDITION 1903
REPRINTED 1912
REPRINTED 1916
REPRINTED 1919
REPRINTED 1952

Published by Susil Gupta for Susil Gupta (India) Ltd.,
35, Chittaranjan Avenue, Calcutta, 12 and Printed by
B. N. Bose at Bose Press, 30, Brojo Mitter Lane, Calcutta.

CONTENTS

CHAPTER VIII

NYAYA AND VAISESHIKA

CHAPTER IX

VAISESHIKA PHILOSOPHY

CHAPTER VIII.

NYAYA AND VAISESHIKA.

Relation between Nyaya and Vaiseshika

WHILE in the systems hitherto examined, particularly in the Vedanta, Samkhya, and Yoga, there runs a strong religious and even poetical vein, we now come to two systems, Nyaya and Vaiseshika, which are very dry and unimaginative, and much more like what we mean by scholastic systems of philosophy, businesslike expositions of what can be known, either of the world which surrounds us or of the world within, that is, of our faculties or powers of perceiving, conceiving, or reasoning on one side, and the objects which they present to us, on the other.

It should be remembered that, like the Samkhya and Yoga, and to a certain extent like the Purva and Uttara-Mimamsa, the Nyaya and Vaiseshika also have by the Hindus themselves been treated as forming but one discipline. We possess indeed a separate body of Nyaya-Sutras and another of Vaiseshika-Sutras, and these with their reputed authors, Gotama and Kanada, have long been accepted as the original sources whence these two streams of the ancient philosophy of India proceeded. But we know now that the literary style which sprang up naturally in what I called the Sutra-period, the period to which the first attempts at a written, in place of a purely mnemonic, literature may have to be ascribed, was by no means restricted to that ancient period, but continued to be so well imitated in later times that we find it used with great success not only in the Samkhya-Sutras, which are later than Madhava (1350 A.D.), but in more modern compositions also. It should always be borne in mind that the Sutras ascribed to Gotama and Kanada presuppose a long previous development of philosophical thought, and instead of regarding the two as two independent streams, it seems far more likely that there existed at first an as yet undifferentiated body of half philosophical half popular thought, bearing on things that can be known, the Padarthas, i.e. *omne scibile,* and on the means of acquiring such knowledge, from which at a later time, according to the preponderance of either the one or the other subject, the two systems of Vaiseshika and Nyaya branched off. These two systems shared of course many things in common, and hence we can well understand that at a later time they should have been drawn together again and treated as one, as we see in Sivaditya's Saptapadarthi (about 1400 A.D.), in the Bhasha-Parichheda, with its commentary the Muktavali, in the Tarkasamgraha, the Tarkakaumudi, the Tarkamrita, &c. For practical purposes it is certainly preferable that we should follow their example and thus avoid the necessity of discussing the same subjects twice over. There may have been an old Tarka, very like our Tarkasamgraha, the one before the bifurcation of the old system of Anvikshiki, the other after the confluence of the two. But these are as yet conjectures only, and may have to remain mere conjectures always, so that, in the present state of our knowledge, and depending, as we have to do, chiefly on the existing Sutras as the authorities recognised in India itself, we must not attempt a historical treatment, but treat each system by itself in spite of unavoidable repetitions.

A very zealous Indian scholar, Mahadeo Rajaram Bodas, in the Introduction to his edition of the Tarkasamgraha, has indeed promised to give us some kind of history of the Nyaya-philosophy in India. But unfortunately that period in the historical development of the Nyaya which is of greatest interest to ourselves, namely that which preceded the composition of the Nyaya-Sutras, had by him also to be left a blank, for the simple reason that nothing is known of Nyaya before Gotama. The later periods, however, have been extremely well treated by Mr. Bodas, and I may refer my readers to him for the best information on the subject. Mr. Bodas places the Sutras of Gotama and Kanada in the fifth or fourth century B.C.; and he expresses a belief that the Vaiseshika, nay even the Samkhya, as systems of thought, were anterior to Buddha, without however adducing any new or certain proofs.

Dignaga

DATES are the weak points in the literary history of India, and, in the present state of our studies, any date, however late, should be welcome. In former years to assign the Kapila-Sutras to the fourteenth or even fifteenth century A.D., would have seemed downright heresy. Was not Kalidasa himself assigned to a period long before the beginning of our era ? It seems now generally accepted that Kalidasa really belonged to the sixth century A.D., and this date of Kalidasa may help us to a date for the Sutras of Gotama, valuable to us, though it may be despised by those who imagine that the value of Sanskrit literature depends chiefly on its supposed remote antiquity. I have pointed out[1] that, according to Indian interpreters, Kalidasa alluded to the logician Dignaga in a verse of his Megha-duta[2]. We may suppose therefore that Dignaga was said by Vachaspati Misra, in his Nyaya-varttika-tatparya-tika, to have interpreted the Nyaya aphorisms of Gotama in a heterodox or Buddhist sense, while Uddyotakara wrote his commentary to refute his interpretation and to restore that of Pakshilasvamin. If Vachaspati Misra is right, we should be allowed to place Dignaga in the sixth century, and assign the same or rather an earlier date to the Sutras of Gotama, as explained by him and other Nyaya philo-sophers. So late a date may not seem to be worth much, still I think it is worth having. Several other dates may be fixed by means of that of Dignaga as I tried to show in the passage quoted above (India, pp. 307 seq.).

A more comprehensive study of Buddhist literature may possibly shed some more light on the chronology of the later literature of the Brahmans, if I am right in supposing that in the beginning the followers of Buddha broke by no means so entirely, as has generally been supposed, with the literary traditions of the Brahmans. It is quite intelligible why among the various systems of Hindu philosophy the Buddhists should have paid little attention to the two Mimamsas, concerned as they both were with the Veda, an authority which the Buddhists had rejected. But there was no reason why the Buddhists should forswear the study of either the Nyaya or Vaiseshika systems, or even the Samkhya system, though making their reserves on

[1] India, p. 307.
[2] See also Prof. Satis Chandra Vidyabhushana in Journal of Buddhist Text Society, IV, parts iii, and iv, p. 16.

certain points, such as the existence of an Isvara, which
was admitted by the Nyayas, but denied by Buddha. We
know that at the court of Harsha, Brahmans, Bauddhas,
and Jainas were equally welcome (India, pp. 307 seq.). We
know from Chinese travellers such as Hiouen-thsang that
Vasubandha, for instance, before he became a Buddhist, had
read with his master, Vinayabhadra or Samghabhadra,[1] not
only the books of the eighteen schools which were Buddhist,
but also the six Tirthya philosophies, clearly meant for the
six Brahmanic systems of philosophy. This Vasubandha,
as a very old man, was actually the teacher of Hiouen-thsang.
who travelled in India from 629 to 648 A.D. Therefore in
Vasubandha's time all the six systems of Indian philosophy
must have been in existence, in the form of Sutras or
Karikas. For we possess, in one case at least, a commentary
by Pakshila-svamin or Vatsyayana on the Nyaya-Sutras.
the same as those which we possess, and we know that the
same Sutras were explained afterwards by Dignaga, the
Buddhist. This Buddhist commentary was attacked by
Uddyotakara, a Brahman, of the sixth century. while in the
beginning of the seventh century Dharmakirtti, a Buddhist,
is said to have defended Dignaga[2] and to have criticised
Uddyotakara's Nyayavarttika. In the ninth century
Dharmottara, a Buddhist, defended Dharmakirtti's and
indirectly Dignaga's interpretation of the Nyaya-Sutras.
and it was not till the tenth century that Vachaspati Misra
finally re-established the Brahmanic view of the Nyaya in
his Nyaya-varttikatatparya-tika. This would coincide with
the period of the Brahmanic reaction and the general
collapse of Buddhism in India, and thus place before us an
intelligible progress in the study of the Nyaya both by
Brahmans and Buddhists. from the sixth to the tenth
century, while the revival of the Nyaya dates from Gamgesa
Upadhyaya who lived in the fourteenth century at Mithila.
    Thanks to the labours of Sarat Chandra Das and Satis
Chandra Vidyabhushana, we have lately gained access to

---

[1] See also Journal of Buddhist Text Society, 1896, p. 16.
[2] Though none of Dignaga's writings have as yet been discovered,
Sri Sarat Chandra states that there is in the library of the Grand Lama
a Tibetan translation of his Nyaya-samuchchaya (Journal of Buddhist
Text Society, part iii, 1896, p. 17).

some of the Sutras of the Buddhist schools of philosophy, which are full of interest. Of the four great schools of the Buddhists, the Madhyamika, Yogachara, Sautrantika, and Vaibhashika, the first or Madhyamika now lies before us in the Madhyamika Vritti by Chandra-Kirtti, and there is every hope that other philosophical treatises also, for instance, the Nyaya-samuchchaya, may be made accessible to us by the labours of these indefatigable scholars.

The Sutras or rather Karikas of the Madhyamika school must, of course, be distinguished from the system of thought which they are meant to explain. The characteristic feature of that system is the Sunya-vada, or nihilism, pure and simple. As such it is referred to and refuted in Gotama's Nyaya-Sutras IV, 37 to 40, in Kapila's Samkhya-Sutras I, 43, 44, in Badarayana's Vedanta-Sutras II, 2, 28, where Samkara distinctly refers the doctrine that we know no objects, but only our perceptions of them, to Sugata or Buddha. The author of the Panchadasi quotes the Madhyamikas by name as the teachers of universal nihilism (Sarvam Sunyam).

If Nagarjuna was really the author of the Madhyamika-Sutras, as we now possess them, they would carry us back to about the first century A.D., and we should have in his Karikas, as explained by Chandra-Kirtti, the oldest document of systematic philosophy in India, which will require very careful examination. Though it is different, no doubt, from all the six systems, it nevertheless shares in common with them many of the ideas and even technical terms. If it teaches the Sunyatva or emptiness of the world, this after all is not very different from the Vedantic Avidya, and the Samkhya Aviveka, and if it teaches the Pratityatva of everything, that need be no more than the dependence of everything on something else.[1] The distinction made by the Madhyamikas between what is Paramarthika, real in the highest sense, and Samvritika, veiled, is much the same as the distinction of the later Vedanta between what is

[1] Pratitya in Pratitya-samutpada and similar words may best be rendered by dependent or conditioned. A son, for instance, is a son, Pitaram Pratitya, dependent on a father, and a father is impossible without a son. In the same way everything is dependent on something else.

really real (Paramarthatah), and what is Vyavaharika, phenomenal or the result of Maya, sometimes called Samriti, the veil that covers the Nirguna Brahman or the Tad, which again is not very different from what the Buddhists meant originally by Sunya, empty, for they hold that even the Sunya is not altogether nothing. Many of the technical terms used by the Madhyamikas are the same as those with which we are acquainted in the other systems. Duhkha, pain, for instance, is divided into Adhyatmika, intrinsic, Adhibhautika, extrinsic, and Adhidaivika, divine or supernatural. We meet with the five perceptions of colour, taste, smell, touch, and sound, and with their five causes, light, water, earth, air, and ether, and we also have the well-known idea that Manas, mind, forms the sixth sense. What is peculiar to the Buddhists is that to them neither the objects of sense nor the sensations point to an underlying substance or reality.

We owe a great debt of gratitude to both Sarat Chandra Das and Sri Satis Chandra Vidyabhushana for their labours in Tibet, and we look forward to many valuable contributions from their pen, more particularly for retranslations from Tibetan.

Whether Buddhist philosophy shares more in common with the Samkhya than with the Nyaya and Vaiseshika seems to me as doubtful as ever. The fundamental position of the Samkhya, as Satkaryavada, is the very opposite of the Buddhist view of the world.

Bibliography

IT was in 1852 that I published my first contributions to a study of Indian philosophy in the *Zeitschrift der Deutschen Morgenlandischen Gesellschaft*. These papers did not extend, however, beyond the Vaiseshika and Nyaya-philosophy as treated in the Tarkasamgraha, and more urgent occupations conected with the edition of the Rig-veda prevented me at the time from finishing what I had prepared for publication on the other systems of Indian philosophy. Though, of course, much new and important material has come to light in the meantime, particularly through the publications of the Vaiseshika-Sutras in the *Bibliotheca Indica*, through the complete translation of them by A. E. Gough, 1873, and through the comprehensive researches of European scholars, such as Professors Deussen and Garbe, I found that there was not much to alter in my old account of Gotama's and Kanada's philosophies, as given in the German Oriental Journal, and in my paper on Indian Logic contributed to the late Archbishop Thomson's Laws of Thought. Indian philosophy has this great advantage that each tenet is laid down in the Sutras with. the utmost precision, so that there can be little doubt as to what Kanada or Gotama thought about the nature of the soul, the reality of human knowledge. the relation between cause and effect, the meaning of creation, and the relation between God or the Supreme Being and man. Thus it may be understood why even papers published so long ago as 1824, such as J. Colebrooke's papers on the Nyaya and Vaiseshika and the other systems of Indian philosophy, may still be recommended to all who want trustworthy information on Indian philosophy. These essays have sometimes been called antiquated, but there is a great difference between what is old and what is antiquated. The difficulty in giving an account of these systems for the benefit of European readers consists far more in deciding what may be safely omitted, so as to bring out the salient points of each system, than in re-capitulating all their tenets.

Books in which the Nyaya and Vaiseshika-systems may be studied by those who are unacquainted with Sanskrit are, besides the papers of Colebrooke:

Ballantyne, The Aphorisms of the Nyaya-Philosophy by Gautama, Sanskrit and English, Allahabad, 1850. (Gautama is the same as Gotama, only that by a tacit agreement Gotama has generally been used as the name of the philosopher, Gautama as that of Buddha, both belonging, it would seem, to the family of the Gautamas or Gotamas, the MSS. varying with regard to the vowel.)

A. E. Gough, The Vaiseshika Aphorisms of Kanada, translated, Benares, 1873.

Manilal Nabubhai Dvivedi, The Tarka-Kaumudi, being an introduction to the principles of the Vaiseshika and Nyaya-philosophies by Laugakshi Bhaskara, Bombay, 1886.

This is the same author to whom we owe a valuable edition of the Yogasara-samgraha.

Windisch, Uber das Nyaya-bhashya, Leipzig, s. a.

Kesava Sastri, The Nyaya-darsana with the commentary of Vatsyayana, in the Pundit, 1877, pp. 60, 109, 311, 363 (incomplete); see also *Bibliotheca Indica*.

Mahadeo Rajaram Bodas. The Tarkasamgraha of Annambhatta, with the author's Dipika and Govardhana's Nyayabodhini, prepared by the late Rao Bahadur Yasavanta Vasadeo Athalya, and published with critical and explanatory notes, Bombay, 1897. This book reached me after these chapters on the Nyaya and Vaiseshika were written, but not too late to enable me to profit by several of his explanations and criticisms, before they were printed.

Nyaya-Philosophy

THOUGH Nyaya has always been translated by logic, we must not imagine that the Nyaya-Sutras are anything like our treatises on formal logic. There is, no doubt, a greater amount of space allowed to logical questions in these than in any of the other systems of Indian philosophy; but originally the name of Nyaya would have been quite as applicable to the Purva-Mimamsa, which is actually called Nyaya in such works, for instance, as Sayana's Nyayamala-vistara, published by Goldstucker. Nor is logic the sole or chief end of Gotama's philosophy. Its chief end, like that of the other Darsanas, is salvation, the *summum bonum* which is promised to all. This *summum bonum* is called by Gotama Nihsreyasa, literally that which has nothing better, the *non plus ultra* of blessedness. This blessedness, according to the ancient commentator Vatsyayana, is described as consisting in renunciation with regard to all the pleasures of this life, and in the non-acceptance of, or indifference to any rewards in the life to come; as being in fact what Brahman is, without fear, without desire, without decay, and without death. Even this Brahmahood must not be an object of desire, for such desire would at once produce a kind of bondage, and prevent that perfect freedom from all fear or hope, which is to follow by itself, but should never be yearned for. This perfect state of freedom, or resignation, can, according to Gotama, be realised in one way only, namely, by knowledge, and in this case, by a knowledge of the sixteen great topics of the Nyaya-philosophy.

Summum Bonum

In this respect all the six systems of philosophy are alike, they always promise to their followers or their believers the attainment of the highest bliss that can he obtained by man.   The approaches leading to that bliss vary, and the character also of the promised bliss is not always the same; yet in each of the six systems philosophy is recommended not, as with us, for the sake of knowledge, but for the highest purpose that man can strive after in this life, that is, his own salvation.

We saw that the Vedanta recognised true salvation or Moksha in the knowledge of Brahman, which knowledge is tantamount to identity with Brahman.   This Brahman or God is, as the Upanishads already declare, invisible, and far beyond the reach of the ordinary faculties of our mind. But he can be learnt from revelation as contained in the Veda, and as Svetaketu was taught ' Tat tvam asi,' ' That art Thou,' every Vedantist is to learn in the end the same lesson, and to realise his identity with Brahman, as the fulfilment of all desires, and the surcease of all suffering (Duhkhanta).

The end of all suffering is likewise the object of the Samkhya-philosophy, though it is to be reached by a different road. Kapila, being a dualist, admits an objective substratum by the side of a subjective spirit or rather spirits, and he sees the cause of all suffering in the spirits' identifying themselves with what is purely objective or material.   He therefore recognises the true means of destroying all bondage and regaining perfect freedom of the spirit in our distinguishing clearly between spirit and matter, between subject and object, between Purusha and Prakriti.   Kaivalya, or aloneness, is the right name for that highest state of bliss which is promised to us by the Samkhya-philosophy.

The Yoga-philosophy. holds much the same view of the soul recovering its freedom, but it insists strongly on certain spiritual exercises by which the soul may best obtain and maintain peace and quietness, and thus free itself effectually from the illusions and sufferings of life. It also lays great stress on devotion to a Spirit, supreme among all the other spirits, whose very existence, according to Kapila, cannot be established by any of the recognised means of real knowledge, the Pramanas.

Of the two Mimamsas we have seen already that the Brahma-Mimamsa or the Vedanta recognises salvation as due to knowledge of the Brahman, which knowledge produces at once the recognition of oneself as in reality Brahman (Brahmavid Brahma eva bhavati, 'He who knows Brahman is Brahman indeed'). It is curious to observe that, while the Samkhya insists on a distinction between Purushas, the subjects, and Prakriti, all that is objective, as the only means of final beatitude, the Vedanta on the contrary postulates the surrendering of all distinction between the Self and the world, and between the Self and Brahman as the right means of Moksha. The roads are different, but the point reached at last is much the same.

The other Mimamsa, that of Jaimini, diverges widely from that of Badarayana. It lays its chief stress on works (Karman) and their right performance, and holds that salvation may be obtained through the performance of such works, if only they are performed without any desire of rewards, whether on earth or in heaven.

Lastly, the Nyaya and Vaiseshika systems, though they also aim at salvation, are satisfied with pointing out the means of it as consisting in correct knowledge, such as can only be obtained from a clear apprehension of the sixteen topics treated by Gotama, or the six or seven categories put forward by Kanada. These two philosophies, agreeing as they do among themselves, seem to me to differ very characteristically from all the others in so far as they admit of nothing invisible or transcendent (Avyakta), whether corresponding to Brahman or to Prakriti. They are satisfied with teaching that the soul is different from the body, and they think that, if this belief in the body as our own is once surrendered, our sufferings, which always reach us through the body, will cease by themselves.

But while we can understand that each of the six systems of Indian philosophy may succeed in removing pain, it is very difficult to see in what that actual happiness was supposed to consist which remained after that removal.

The Vedanta speaks of Ananda, or bliss, that resides in the highest Brahman ; but the happiness to be enjoyed by the souls near the throne of Brahman, and in a kind of paradise, is not considered as final, but is assigned to a lower class only. That paradise has no attraction, and would give no real satisfaction to those who have reached the knowledge of the Highest Brahman. Their blissful knowledge is described as oneness with Brahman, but no details are added. The bliss held out by the Samkhyas also is very vague and indefinite. It can arise only from the Purusha himself, if left entirely to himself, far from all the illusions and disturbances arising from objective nature, or the works of Prakriti.

Lastly, the Apavarga (bliss) of the Nyaya and Vaiseshika systems seems entirely negative, and produced simply by the removal of false knowledge. Even the different names given to the supreme bliss promised by each system of philosophy tell us very little. Mukti and Moksha mean deliverance, Kaivalya, isolation or detachment, Nihsreyasa, *non plus ultra*, Amrita, immortality, Apavarga, delivery. Nor does the well-known Buddhist term Nirvana help us much. We know indeed from Panini (VIII, 2, 50) that the word was pre-Buddhistic and existed in his time. He tells us that, if used in the sense of 'blown out,' the right form would be Nirvatah, such as Nirvato vatah, ' the wind has ceased to blow,' but Nirvano-jnih, 'the fire is gone out.' We cannot prove, however, that Nirvana was used as the technical term for the *summum bonum* in Panini's time, and it does not seem to occur in the classical Upanishads. Its occurring as the title of one of the modern Upanishads makes it all the more likely that it was borrowed there from Buddhistic sources. There is one passage only, in the shorter text of the Maitreya[1] Upanishad where Nirvanam anusasanam occurs, possibly meant for Nirvananusasanam, the teaching of Nirvana. What should be clearly understood is that in the early Buddhistic writings also, Nirvana does not yet mean a complete blow-

---

[1] Sacred Books of the East, XV, p. 61.

ing out of the individual soul, but rather the blowing out
and subsiding of all human passions and the peace and
quietness which result from it. The meaning of complete
annihilation was a later and purely philosophical meaning
attached to Nirvana, and no one certainly could form an
idea of what that Nirvana was meant to be in the Buddhist
Nihilistic or Sunyata-philosophy.   I doubt even whether
the Upanishads could have given us a description of what
they conceived their highest Mukti or perfect freedom to
be. In fact they confess themselves (Taitt. Up. II, 4, 1)
that 'all speech turns away from the bliss of Brahman,
unable to reach it',' and when language fails, thought is not
likely to fare better.

Means of Salvation

TURNING now to the means by which the Nyaya-philosophy undertakes to secure the attainment of the *summum
bonum* or Apavarga, we find them enumerated in the
following list:

The Sixteen Topics or Padarthas

(1) Pramana, means of knowledge; (2) Prameya, objects
of knowledge; (3) Samsaya, doubt; (4) Prayojana, purpose; (5) Drishtanta, instance; (6) Siddhanta, established
truth; (7) Avayava, premisses; (8) Tarka, reasoning; (9)
Nirnaya, conclusion; (10) Vada, argumentation; (11) Jalpa,
sophistry; (12) Vitanda, wrangling. cavilling; (13) Hetva-
bhasa, fallacies; (14) Chhala, quibbles; (15) Jati, false
analogies; (16) Nigrahasthana, unfitness for arguing.

This may seem a very strange list of the topics to be
treated by any philosophy, particularly by one that claims
the title of Nyaya or logic.   It is clear that in reality
the chapters on Pramana or means of knowledge, and
Prameya, objects of knowledge, comprehend the whole of
philosophy.

Means of Knowledge

THE four Pramanas, according to Gotama, are Pratyaksha,

---

[1] See a very learned article on Nirvana by Professor Satis Chandra
Vidyabhushana, in the Journal of the Buddhist Text Society, VI,
part i, p. 22.

sensuous perception, Anumana, inference, Upamana, comparison, and Sabda, word.

Perception comes first, because inference can only begin to do its work after perception has prepared the way, and has supplied the materials to which inference can be applied. Comparison is no more than a subordinate kind of inference, while the Sabda or the word, particularly that of the Veda, depends again, as we should say, on a previous inference by which the authority of the word, more particularly the revealed word, has first been established. Imperfect as this analysis of our instruments of knowledge may seem, it seems to me highly creditable to Indian philosophers that they should have understood the necessity of such an analysis on the very threshold of any system of philosophy. How many misunderstandings might have been avoided if all philosophers had recognised the necessity of such an introductory chapter. If we must depend for all our knowledge, first on our senses, then on our combinatory and reasoning faculties, the question whether revelation falls under the one or the other, or whether it can claim an independent authority, can far more easily be settled than if such questions are not asked in *limine*, but turn up casually whenever transcendental problems come to be treated.

Objects of Knowledge

THE objects of knowledge, as given by the Nyaya, comprehend *omne scibile*, such as body, soul, organs of sense, qualities, cognition, mind, will, fault, death, enjoyment, pain, and final freedom. These objects are afterwards discussed singly, but have of course little to do with logic. Doubt and purpose mark the first steps towards philosophical discussion, instances and established truths supply materials, while premisses and reasoning lead on to the conclusion which disputants wish to reach. From Nos. 10 to 16, we have rules for dialectic rather than for logic. We are taught how to meet the artifices of our antagonists in a long argumentation, how to avoid or to resist sophistry, wrangling, fallacies, quibbles, false analogies, and downright misstatements, in fact, how to defend truth against unfair antagonists.

If from our point of view we deny the name of logic to such problems, we should be perfectly justified, though a glance at the history of Greek philosophy would show us that, before logic became an independent branch of philosophy it was likewise mixed up with dialectic and with questions of some more special interest, the treatment of which led gradually to the elaboration of general rules of thought, applicable to all reasoning, whatever its subject may be.

It is quite clear that these sixteen topics should on no account be rendered, as they mostly have been, by the sixteen categories. Categories are the *praedicabilia*, or whatever can be predicated, and however much the meaning of this term may have been varied by European philosophers, it could never have been so far extended as to include wrangling, fallacies, quibbles and all the rest. We shall see that the six or seven Padarthas of the Vaiseshikas correspond far more nearly to the categories of the Aristotelian and afterwards of European philosophy in general.

Padartha, Object

NOTHING shows so well the philosophical character of the Sanskrit language as this very word Padartha, which has been translated by category. It means in ordinary Sanskrit simply a thing, but literally it meant Artha, the meaning, the object, Pada, of a word. What we should call objects of thought, they called far more truly objects of words, thus showing that from the earliest times they understood that no thought was possible except in a word, and that the objects of our knowledge became possible only after they had been named. Their language passed through an opposite process to that of Latin. Latin called every kind of knowledge or all known things *gnomina*, from *gnosco*, to know; but after a time, and after the initial *g* had been dropped, as we drop it involuntarily in *gnat*, their *gnomina* became *nomina*, and were then supposed to be something different from the old and forgotten *gnomina* ; they became *nomina*, i.e. mere names.

Six Padarthas of Vaiseshika

ACCORDING to the Vaiseshikas, we have six Padarthas, i.e. six general meanings, categories or predicates, to which

all words i.e. all things can be referred. All known things
must be either substances (9), qualities (24), or motions,
the last meaning, however. more than mere local move-
ment, so as to correspond in fact to our activity or even
to our becoming (Werden). Knowledge (Buddhi) is here
treated as one of the qualities of the soul, which itself is
one of the substances, so that many things which with us
belong to psychology and logic, are treated by the Vaiseshikas under this head.

The next two, the general and the particular, comprehend what is shared in common by many objects, and
what is peculiar to one, and thus distinguishes it from all
others.

Samavaya or intimate connection is a very useful name
for a connection between things which cannot exist one
without the other, such as cause and effect, parts and the
whole, and the like. It comes very near to the Avina-
bhava, i.e. the Not-without-being, and should be carefully
distinguished from mere conjunction or succession.

The seventh category, Abhava, or negation, was added,
it would seem, at a later time, and can be applied to previous, to present or to subsequent non-existence. or even
to absolute Abhava.

Madhava's Account of Nyaya

In order to see what, in the eyes of native scholars, the
Nyaya-philosophy was meant to achieve, it may be useful
to look at an account of it given by the great Madhava-
charya in his Sarvadarsana-samgraha, the compendium of
all the systems of philosophy. 'The Nyaya-sastra,' he says,
'consists of five books, and each book contains two daily
portions or Ahnikas. In the first Ahnika of the first book
the venerable Gotama discusses the definitions of nine
subjects, beginning with "proof" (Pramana), and in the
second those of the remaining seven, beginning with discussion (Vada). In the first daily portion of the second
book he examines doubt (8), discusses the four kinds of
proof, and refutes all objections that could be made against
their being considered as instruments of right knowledge;
and in the second he shows that "presumption" and other
Pramanas are really included in the four kinds of "proof"

already given. In the first daily portion of the third book
he examines the soul, the body, the senses, and their
objects; in the second, "understanding" (Buddhi) and
mind (Manas). In the first daily portion of the fourth
book he examines activity (Pravritti), faults (Dosha),
transmigration (Pretyabhava), fruit or reward (Phala),
pain (Duhkha), and final liberation (Apavarga); in the
second he investigates the truth as to the causes of the
"faults," and also the subject of "wholes" and "parts."
In the first daily portion of the fifth book he discusses the
various kinds of futility (Jati), and in the second the
various kinds of objectionable proceedings (Nigrahasthana).[1]

After having held out in the first Sutra the promise of
eternal salvation to all who study his philosophy properly,
Gotama proceeds at once to a description of the steps by
which the promised Nihsreyasa, or highest happiness, is to
be attained, namely by the successive annihilation of false
knowledge, of faults, of activity, and, in consequence, of
birth and suffering. When the last or suffering has been
annihilated there follows *ipso facto* freedom, or blessedness
(Apavarga), literally abstersion or purification. This process reminds us strongly of some of the links in the Patichcha
Samuppada of the Buddhists. This is generally translated
by Chain of Causation, and was meant to sum up the causes
of existence or of misery, the twelve Nidanas. It really
means origin resting on something else. The first step is
Avidya or that cosmic Nescience which was so fully elaborated in the Vedanta-philosophy. According to the Buddhists there follow on Avidya the Samkharas[1], all the
varieties of existence; on these Vijnana, sensation; on this
Namarupa, names and forms; on these the Shadayatana,
the six organs of perception. Then follow in succession
Sparsa, contact, Vedana, sensation, Trishna, desire, Upa-
dana, attachment, Bhava, state of existence, Jati, birth,
Jaramarana, decay and death, Soka, sorrow, Parideva,
lamentation, Duhkha, suffering, Daurmanasya, grief, and
Upayasa, despair[2].

This chain of successive states proclaimed by Buddha

[1] Cf. Garbe, Samkhya-Philosophie, p. 299 seq.
[2] Cf. Childers, s.v.

has formed the subject of ever so many commentaries, none of which seems quite satisfactory. The chain of Gotama is shorter than that of Gautama, but the general likeness can hardly be mistaken. Who was the earlier of the two, Gotama or Gautama, is still a contested question, but whatever the age of our Sutras (the sixteen topics) may be, a Nyaya-philosophy existed clearly before the rise of Buddhism.

I. Pramana

Gotama proceeds next to examine each of the sixteen topics.

The first topic or Padartha is Pramana, which is said to consist of four kinds, all being means or measures of knowledge. They are in the Nyaya as in the Vaiseshika, (1) Pratyaksha, sense-perception; (2) Anumana, inference; (3) Upamana, comparison; and (4) Sabda, word.

Perception or Pratyaksha

1. Perception (Pratyaksha) is explained as knowledge produced by actual contact between an organ of sense and its corresponding object, this object being supposed to be real. How a mere passive impression, supposing the contiguity of the organs of sense with outward objects had once been established, can be changed into a sensation or into a presentation (*Vorstellung*), or what used to be called a material idea, is a question not even asked by Gotama.

Inference or Anumana

2. Inference (Anumana), preceded by perception, is described as of three kinds, Purvavat, proceeding from what was before, i.e. an antecedent; Seshavat, proceeding from what was after, i.e. a consequent; and Samanyato Drishta, proceeding from what is constantly seen together. Though, as we saw, Charvaka rejects every kind of Anumana or inference, he, as Vachaspati Misra remarks very acutely (Karika 5), in attacking his antagonists for their mistaken faith in inference, does really himself rely on inference, without which he could not so much as surmise that his antagonists held erroneous opinions, such erroneous opinions

being never brought into contact with his organs of sense, but being supposed to exist on the strength of Anumana.

The meaning of the three kinds of inference differs considerably according to different commentators. It is generally explained that a Purvavat, preceded by or possessed of a prius, refers to the mutual relation between a sign and what is signified by it, so that the observation of the sign leads to the observation or rather inference of what is universally associated with it or marked by it. This unconditoinal association is afterwards treated under the name of Vyapti, literally pervasion of one thing by another. Examples will make this clearer. When we see a river rising we infer as its Purva or *prius* that it has rained. When we see that the ants carry their eggs, or that the peacocks are screaming, we infer as the Sesha or posterior that it will rain (Nyaya S. 11, 5, 37). It is true that in all these cases the reason given for an inference may, as it is called, wander away, that is, may prove too much or too little. In that case the fault arises from the conditioned character of the Vyapti or the pervasion. Thus the rising of a river may be due to its having been dammed up, the carrying off their eggs by the ants may have been caused by some accidental disturbance of their hill, and the screaming of the peacocks may really have been imitated by men. The fault, however, in such cases does not affect the process of inference, but the Vyapti only; and as soon as the relation between the sign and the thing signified has been rectified, the inference will come right. Each Vyapti, that is each inductive truth, consists of a sign (Linga), and the bearer of a sign (Lingin). The bearer of the sign is called Vyapaka or pervading, the sign itself Vyapya, what is to be pervaded. Thus smoke is the sign (Linga, Vyapya), and fire is what pervades the smoke, is always present when there is smoke, is the *sine qua non* of smoke, is therefore Lingin or Vyapaka.

But everything depends on whether the two are either absolutely or only conditionally related. These conditions are called the Upadhis. Thus the relation between fire and smoke is conditioned by damp firewood; and there are other cases also where fire exists without smoke, as in a red-hot iron ball.

The third kind of inference, the Samanyato Drishta, based on what is constantly seen together, is illustrated by our inferring that the sun is moving because it is seen in different places, everything that is seen in different places being known to have moved. Here the Vyapti, on which the ancient logicians depended, had to wait till it was corrected by Copernicus.

Even a deaf man may infer the existence of sound if he sees a particular conjunction of a drumstick with a drum. It requires but a certain amount of experience to infer the presence of an ichneumon from seeing an excited snake, or to infer fire from perceiving the heat of water, nay to infer the existence of an organ of touch from our feeling any animated body. In all such cases the correctness of the inference is one thing, the truth of the conclusion quite another, the latter being always conditioned by the presence or absence of certain Upadhis.

Different from this very natural explanation of the three kinds of Anumana is another, according to which Sesha is not supposed to mean subsequent effect, allowing us to infer its invariable cause, but is to be taken in the sense of what is left. This is illustrated by an example, such as 'Earth is different from all other elements, because it alone possesses the quality of smell,' that is to say, earth is left over, being separated from all other elements by its peculiar quality of smell. One might have inferred from the fact that the element of earth possesses smell, that all elements possessed the same. But this is wrong, because it is Aprasakta, i.e. does not apply. It would be no better than if we were to infer that smell must belong to other qualities and actions also, which would be simply absurd. But as earth is different from all other substances, we may infer that smell does not belong to anything that is not earth, except artificially, as in scented articles. This is the residuary inference, or method of residues.

In the same manner we are told that Purva, the *prius*, should not be taken in the sense of antecedent cause, but as a general concept the properties of which have been formerly comprehended as known. Thus from smoke on a hill we should infer the presence of a particular fire on the hill, falling under the general concept of fire as belonging to the genus fire.

The third, or Samanyato Drishta, inference, is illustrated by our inferring the existence of senses, which are by themselves imperceptible (Indriyani Atindriyani), because we do perceive colour &c., and as no actions can take place without instruments we may infer the existence of senses as instruments for our action of seeing, &c. Samanyato Drishta thus becomes very like the seeing of a general concept. It is inference from the sensible to the supersensible.

With all respect for Indian commentators, both ancient and modern, I must confess that I prefer the more natural explanation of the three kinds of inference being based on cause, effect, and association, nay I find it difficult to understand why this view should have been given up by the modern Naiyayikas.

Among these three inferences, the first and last are called Vita or straightforward, the second Avita, or not straightforward; but this only if we adopt the second explanation of the three kinds of Anumana.

We shall have to deal again with Anumana when we come to consider the seventh Padartha, the Avayavas or Premisses, or what we should call the members of a syllogism.

Comparison or Upamana

3. Next follows Comparison (Upamana) or recognition of likeness, explained as an instrument for ascertaining what has to be ascertained by means of similarity with something well known before. For instance, having been told that a Gavaya (*bos gavaeus*) is like a cow, and seeing an animal like a cow, but not a cow, a man may infer that it is a Gavaya.

Word or Sabda

4. WORD (Sabda) is explained either as a precept of one worthy to be trusted, or as a right precept. It refers, we are told, either to visible or invisible objects. It is curious to see that among the people to be trusted (Apta) the commentator should mention not only Rishis and Aryas, but

·Mlechhas or barbarians also, provided they are well in-
formed.   Strictly speaking the Veda would not come under
Sabda, unless it can be proved to be Aptavachana, the word
of one worthy to be trusted.

II. Prameya

THE second Padartha or topic is Prameya, that is, all that
can be established by the four Pramanas, or what we
should call *omne scibile*. Twelve such objects are mentioned: (1) Self or soul, (2) body, (3) senses, (4) sense-
objects, (5) understanding, (6) mind, (7) activity (will),
(8) faults, (9) transmigration, (10) rewards of deeds,
(11) suffering, (12) final beatitude. The first six of these
are called causative, the other six caused.   Gotama next proceeds to define each of these Prameyas, by enumerating the
characteristics peculiar to each.

1.   The characteristics of the Self are desire, hatred, will,
pleasure, pain, and knowing (Buddhi).

2.   Body is defined as the seat of action, of the senses, and
what they intimate, that is, their objects[1].

3.   The senses or organs of sense are defined as those of
smell, taste, sight, touch, and hearing.   They are supposed
to arise from the elements.

4.   These elements (from which the senses draw their
origin and their perceptions) are earth, water, light, air,
and ether; while the objects of the senses are the qualities
of earth, &c., such as odour, savour, colour, touch, and
sound.   It is essential to remember that of the elements
the first four are both eternal and non-eternal, while the
fifth, Akasa, which we translate by ether, is eternal only,
and hence not tangible.   The non-eternal substances are
either inorganic, organic, or sensitive, but always related
to the sense, so that the sense of light perceives or sees
light only.   The sense of scent perceives odour only, and
so on.

5.   As to Buddhi, understanding, it is by the Naiyayikas
explained as being the same as apprehension or knowledge.

---

[1] According to the commentary the sensations, and according to the
next Sutra, the qualities of the objects of sense, which alone can be
perceived.

and as being twofold, notion, Anubhava, and remembrance. Smarana.

5. Mind (Manas) is different from understanding, and is explained as that which prevents more than one notion from arising at the same time, that is to say, it prevents the rushing in of all sorts of sensuous impressions at once, and regulates them in our consciousness. It is sometimes called the gatekeeper or controller of the senses. The transformation of sensations into percepts, and of percepts into concepts, a subject little cultivated by Indian philosophers, would naturally fall to the Manas. Little attention, however, is paid by Hindu logicians to this subject, which has assumed such large proportions with us. Even the distinction between percepts, *Vorstellungen*, and concepts, *Begriffe*, has never been fully realised by Indian logicians.

Manas or mind is considered as Anu or an atom, and the question has been fully discussed how Manas, being Anu, can be united with Atman, which is Vibhu, or infinitely great. If, with the Mimamsakas, it were admitted that the two could unite, then there could never be any cessation of knowledge, such as we know there is in sleep, for the union of Atman and Manas, if once effected, would be indissoluble. It is held by the Naiyayikas that when Manas enters a particular region of the body called Puritat, the effect of the union of Atman and Manas is neutralised, and sleep ensues. If Manas were supposed to be co-extensive with the body it would be Anitya, non-eternal, and be destroyed with the body, and we should lose that which retains the impressions of acts done in the body, nay we should be unable to account for a future life and the inequalities of birth in any future life; we should have to admit, in fact, effects without a cause. The Naiyayikas hold, therefore, that the Manas is both Anu, infinitely small, and Nitya, eternal (Tarka-kaumudi, p. 4, n. 24), while Manas, like Atman, is eternal and numerous, differing, however, from Atman by being atomic in dimension.

7. Activity (will) is the effort of body, of the understanding working through the mind (Manas), and of the voice.

8. Faults cause acts, and acts bear fruit, good or bad[1].

9. Pretyabhava is transmigration.

10. Rewards are results produced by faults, in the most general sense, and by actions, consequent on them, so that they are sometimes explained as consciousness of pleasure and pain.

11. Pain is characterised by vexation; and as pleasure also involves pain, both pain and pleasure are here treated together under pain. Entire deliverance from pain and pleasure is

12. Apavarga or final beatitude.

Having thus examined all that can form the object of our knowledge, the Pramanas or measures of knowledge, and the Prameyas, we now enter on the third of the sixteen topics.

III. Samsaya

SAMSAYA or doubt. Doubt, we are told, arises from our recognition of various attributes opposed to one another in one and the same object, as when we recognise in a distant object the qualities of a man and of a post. The definition given of doubt shows that the ancient logicians of India had carefully thought about the different causes of doubt, so that they were led to the admission of three or even five kinds of it.   •

IV. Prayojana. V. Drishtanta. VI. Siddhanta

BUT these disquisitions, as well as those referring to (IV) Prayojana, purpose or motive; (V) Drishtanta, example, familiar case; (VI) Siddhanta, tenets, contain nothing that is of peculiar interest to the historian of philosophy, except so far as they offer once more the clearest evidence of a long continued previous study of logic in the ancient schools or settlements of India.

VII. The Avayavas, or Members of a Syllogism

MUCH more important is the next subject, the so-called members, that is, the members of a syllogism. To us a

---

[1] See I, 20, Pravrittidoshajanitarthah phalam.

syllogism and its structure are so familiar that we hardly feel surprised at meeting with it in the schools of logic in India. Yet, unless we are inclined to admit either an influence of Greek on Indian, or of Indian on Greek philosophy, neither of which has as yet been proved, the coincidences between the two are certainly startling. As to myself I feel bound to confess that I see no evidence of any direct influence, either on one side or on the other; and though I am far from denying its possibility, I keep to my conviction, expressed many years ago, that we must here also admit the existence of undesigned coincidences to a much larger extent than our predecessors were inclined to do. We must never forget that what has been possible in one country, is possible in another also.

At the time when the different systems of Indian philosophy became first known to the scholars of Europe everything that came from the East was looked upon as of extreme antiquity. There had been vague traditions of ancient Indian philosophy even before the time of Aristotle. Alexander himself, we are told, was deeply impressed with that idea, as we may gather from his desire to communicate with the gymnosophists of India.

Indian and Greek Logic

ONE of these gymnosophists or Digambaras seems to have been the famous Kalanos (Kalyana?), who died a voluntary death by allowing himself to be burnt before the eyes of the Macedonian army. It was readily admitted, therefore, by European scholars that the Hindu systems of philosophy, and particularly Indian Logic, were more ancient than that of Aristotle, and that the Greeks had borrowed the first elements of their philosophy from the Hindus.

The view that Alexander might actually have sent some Indian philosophical treatises to his tutor at home, and this even at a time when, as far as we know at present, manuscripts in India were still unknown, and that Aristotle might have worked them up into a system, inconceivable as it now seems to us, was taken up and warmly defended by men like Gorres and others. Gorres undertook to prove that the Greeks had actually retained some technical terms taken from Sanskrit. For instance, as

Indian philosophers admit five elements, the fifth being called Akasa, ether, Gorres, without giving any reference, quoted a passage from Aristotle in which he speaks of a fifth element and calls it *akat-onomaton*, i.e. *akas-nominatum*, this being probably an ingenious conjecture for *akatonomaston*.[1] It is quite true that one such verbal coincidence would settle the whole question, but even that one coincidence has not yet been discovered. No doubt there were many points of coincidence between Greek and Indian logic, but none in technical terms, which like proper names in Comparative Mythology, would have clinched the argument once for all.

But does it, on the other hand, show a higher power of historical criticism, if Niebuhr and others stood up for the opposite view and tried to derive Indian philosophy from Greece? Niebuhr is reported to have said in his Lectures on Ancient History, 'If we look at Indian philosophy we discern traces of a great similarity with that of the Greeks. Now as people have given up the hypothesis that Greek philosophy formed itself after Indian philosophy, we cannot explain this similarity except by the intercourse which the Indians had with the Graeco-Macedonic kingdom of Bactra.'

Is that really so? To Niebuhr and to most Greek scholars it would naturally seem next to impossible that Greek philosophy, which can be watched from its first childhood, should have been of foreign origin, a mere importation from India. They know how Greek philosophy grew up gradually, how its growth ran parallel with the progress of Grecian poetry, religion, art, and civilisation. They feel it to be a home-grown production, as certainly as Plato and Aristotle were Greeks and not Brahmans.

But they ought not to be surprised if Sanskrit scholars have just the same feeling with regard to Indian philosophy. They also can show how in India the first philosophical ideas, as yet in a very vague and shadowy form, show themselves in the hymns of the early poets of the Veda. They can trace their gradual development in the Brahmanas

[1] Plutarch, De Placit. Philos, quotes Epicurus as to the soul being a mixture of three elements, fire, air, and water, and a fourth *akatonomaston ho en auto aisthetikon*.

and Upanishads. They can show how they gave rise to discussions, public and private, how they assumed a more and more definite form, and how at last they were fixed in different schools in that form in which they have reached us. They, too, are as certain that philosophy was autochthonous in India as that Gotama and Kanada were Brahmans and not Greeks.

What then remains? It seems to me that until it can be proved *historically* that the Greeks could freely converse with Indians in Greek or in Sanskrit on metaphysical subjects or *vice versa*, or until technical philosophical terms can be discovered in Sanskrit of Greek, or in Greek of Sanskrit origin, it will be best to accept facts and to regard both Greek and Indian philosophy as products of the intellectual soil of India and of Greece, and derive from their striking similarities this simple conviction only, that in philosophy also there is a wealth of truth which forms the common heirloom of all mankind, and may be discovered by all nations if they search for it with honesty and perseverance.

Having once learnt this lesson we shall feel less inclined, whenever we meet with coincidences of any kind, to conclude at once that they cannot be explained except by admitting a historical contact and a borrowing on one side or the other[1]. No doubt there are the Vaiseshika categories=Padarthas, there is Dravya, substance, Guna, quality; there is genus=Samanya, and species=Visesha, nay, even syllogism=the Avayavas; there is induction=Vyapti, and deduction=Upanaya, both in Sanskrit and in Greek. But why not? If they could be developed naturally in Greece, why not in India? Anyhow, we must wait and not hamper the progress of research by premature assertions.

VIII. Tarka

But before we enter into the intricacies of the Indian syllogism, it will be best to finish first what remains of the sixteen topics of the Nyaya. After the five members follows VIII, Tarka, which is explained as refutation, or reasoning from the fitness of the case, as when a person,

---

[1] See M. M., On Coincidences, a paper read before the Royal Society of Literature, 1896.

though seeing smoke on a hill, does not see that there
must be fire, and is thereupon made to see that if the hill
were without fire, it would of necessity be without smoke.
It is meant to be a *reductio ad absurdum*.

IX. Nirnaya

THE next topic to be considered is IX, Nirnaya, ascer-
tainment.

X-XVI. Vada, Galpa, Vitanda, Hetvabhasa, Jati, Chhala, Nigrahasthana

THEN follow the paragraphs connected with rhetoric or
eristics rather than with logic, such as X, Vada or argumentation, consisting of objections and answers, both disputants, however, caring for truth only; next XI, Galpa,
sophistical wrangling or attacking what has been established, by means of fraud; XIV, Jati, futility, arising from
false analogies; XV, Chhala, quibbling; and XVI, Nigrahasthana, unfitness for discussion. In the last five cases
disputants are supposed to care for victory only, and not
for truth.

If this wrangling is devoid of any attempt at really
establishing an opposite opinion, it is called XII, Vitanda,
cavilling.

We next come to XIII, Hetvabhasas, or specious arguments, that is, paralogisms and sophisms. These are
Savyabhichara, arguments that prove too much, Viruddha,
that prove the reverse, Prakaranasama, that tell equally on
both sides, Sadhyasama, that stand themselves in need of
proof, and Kalatita, mistimed.

As to XV, Chhala, fraud in using words in a sense
different from what is generally understood, and XIV, Jati,
futility arising from change of class, they have been mentioned before. It is difficult to understand why Jati, i.e.
birth or genus, should mean a futile argument, unless it
meant originally a *transitio in alterum genus*, as when, in
answer to an argument that a man is unable to travel,
because he has a fever, it should be answered that he is
able to travel, because he is a soldier. Here the same man
is referred first to the class of those who suffer from

fever, and then to that of soldiers who are always supposed
to be able to march.

The last, XVI, Nigrahasthana, unfitness for discussion, is
when a man by misunderstanding or not understanding, yet
continuing to talk, renders himself liable to reproof.

This may seem a long list, though in several cases there
are subdivisions which have here been left out, and yet at
the end of the list Gotama actually apologises and says
that there are many more sorts of futility, &c., which have
been passed over by him, but will have to be discussed
hereafter.

Judgments on Indian Logic

If we were to look upon this list of the sixteen topics, as
some have done, as an abstract of Gotama's whole philosophy, or with others, as his table of the categories,
European philosophers would no doubt be justified in saying
what Ritter said in his History of Philosophy that the exposition of the Nyaya is tedious, loose, and unmethodical.
It is certainly mixed up with subjects which have nothing
to do with pure logic, but so was Greek logic in its beginning, in the school of Zeno, for instance. It may be also
too minute for our taste, but it cannot be called loose at the
same time. It is equally unfair to charge the Nyaya and
all the other systems of Indian philosophy, with being un-
practical and with entirely ignoring all the problems of
ethics. We must remember that philosophy in India had
very different antecedents from what it had with us. We
ourselves can hardly conceive a philosophy which in the
end is not to be of practical usefulness, and which ignores
all questions of morality. But we must learn to take philosophers as they are. Morality with the Brahmans depends
either on prescriptive sacra (Dharma), or on what is called
Samaya, the agreement of good people. But its strongest
support is a firm belief in the solidarity of life here and
hereafter, and a firm conviction that nothing can ever be
lost. The popular mind of India seems never to have
doubted the fact that every good or every evil thought
or deed will grow and bear fruit, and that no one can
ever escape from the consequences of his own acts and
thoughts. Whether such a belief is right or wrong is not

the question, but it produced at all events a deep sense of responsibility. Instead of complaints about the injustice and cruelty of God, people were taught that what seemed undeserved misfortunes, were fully deserved, were in fact the natural consequences of previous acts, and in one respect the safest means of paying off all debts. Philosophy at the same time held out a hope that in the end this net of consequences might be broken through, and the Self, enlightened by true knowledge, return to whence it came, return to himself and be himself; that is, be again the Universal Self, free for ever from the chains and pains of this transient episode of life on earth.

That highest freedom and beatitude, according to Indian views, depended on philosophy or knowledge; it could not be acquired by good works or good thoughts alone. This again may be right or wrong, but I can discover no looseness of reasoning in it, nor in Indian philosophy in general. We must not forget that, from a Hindu point of view, this life on earth is but an episode that may be very important in itself, but is a mere nothing compared with what lies behind and before, the eternal life of the soul. If they hold that a knowledge of the true relation between man and the world, and between man and the Author of the world, is essential to true freedom and true happiness, are they so far wrong? And what is true in the case of the Vedanta, the Samkhya and Yoga systems of philosophy, is true in a certain sense of the Nyaya also. It may be said that the fundamental points of this philosophy are contained in what can be known, Prameya, and the means of knowing, Pramana, that is to say, it seemed necessary to Gotama to establish, first of all, the limits of the two, just as Kant began his philosophy with his Critique of Pure Reason, that is, the tracing of the limits of Pure Reason. But this being done in full detail under his sixteen headings, Gotama too, like Badarayana and Kapila, enters on an explanation of the process by which it was possible to destroy ignorance or Mithyajnana, which, as he holds, is the true cause of error or sin, 'which is the cause of activity, which is the cause of birth, which is the cause of suffering' (I, 2). This, whether right or wrong, is at all events perfectly coherent, nor does it betray any looseness of reasoning, if indirectly the whole Nyaya-philosophy is called the cause of final freedom or blessedness. Modern Nyaya is almost entirely confined to Pramana.

The Later Books of the Nyaya

IN this way the first book of the Nyaya-Sutras gives us indeed a fair outline of the whole of Gotama's philosophy, while the following three books enter into a more minute examination of its details. Thus the second book treats more fully of the Pramanas, the third and fourth of the Prameyas, the fifth treats of all that comes under the head of paralogisms. Some of the questions discussed in these books show quite clearly that they must have formed the subject of lively and long-continued controversy, for though some of the objections raised may seem to us of little importance, they prove at all events the conscientiousness of the early Naiyayikas.

Pratyaksha, Perception

THAT sensuous perception should be a Pramana or authority would hardly seem to us to have required further proof. But Gotama or his opponent starts the question, on what ground the evidence of the senses can claim such authority, or who is the authority of its authority. This is an idea that anticipates an important element of modern philosophy. As a balance may serve to weigh a thing, but must also be weighed or tested itself, it might be said that the authority of the senses also requires to be established by another authority, and so on *ad infinitum*. In answer to this Gotama uses what seems to be an *ad hominem* argument, namely, that if there is no authority anywhere, there can be none on the side of the objector either. The objector would cut away the ground under his own feet, and thus would himself have no *locus standi* for offering any objections (II, 13).

But admitting that sensuous perception has authority just as a lamp has light to light up the things around it, the next question is whether the definition of sensuous perception, that which results from contact of sense with its object, is not incomplete, because for real 'perception

there must be contact not only with the organs of sense,
but likewise between the senses and the mind (Manas), and
between the mind and the Self (Atman). This is not
denied by Gotama, he only defends himself by saying that
everything cannot be said at the same time, and that his
definition of perception, though it dwells only on what is
essential (the contact of sense and object), does by no
means exclude that between mind and Self, on the contrary
takes it here for granted. He also admits that contact
between sense and object does not invariably produce
perception, that in fact there may be sensation without
perception, as when we are so absorbed in listening to music
that we do not perceive the objects around us, from want
of attention. This again reminds us of modern philosophy.
Even such questions as to whether there is any interval of
time between our hearing the sound of a word and our
realising its meaning, are alluded to by Gotama and his
school, and the question whether several impressions can be
taken in at the same time is negatived by a reference to the
running of a pin through a number of sheets of a MS.
Here the piercing seems simultaneous, yet we know that it
can only be successive. Another question also which has
lately occupied our psycho-physiologists, whether perception
does not involve inference, is discussed by Gotama (II, 31),
particularly in cases where our senses can apprehend a part
only of their object when perceiving, for instance, a tree.
of which one side only can be seen at the time, while the
rest has to be supplied by memory or inference. This leads
him on to another question whether there really is such a
thing as a whole, and as we can in reality never see more
than one side at a time, he tries to account for the process
by which we take a part for the whole. No one, for instance,
has ever seen more than one side of the moon, yet taking
it as a whole, and as a globe, we postulate and are con-
vinced that there is another side also. The illustration
given by Gotama to show that a tree is a whole, namely,
because when we shake one branch of it, the whole tree
trembles, may seem childish to us, but it is exactly in these
simple and so-called childish thoughts that the true interest
of ancient philosophy seems to me to consist.

Time—Present, Past, Future

THE next problem that occupies Gotama is that of time—
of present, past, and future. The objector, and in this
case, it seems, a very real objector, for it is the opinion of
the Buddhists, denies that there is such a thing as present
time, because the moment we see a fruit falling from a tree,
we see only that it has fallen or that it has still to fall, but
never that it is falling. Here the answer is that past and
future themselves would be impossible, if the present did
not exist, and on the objector's admitting such a possibility,
Gotama remarks that in that case perception and all that
springs from it would be altogether impossible, because it
can only depend on what is present.

Upamana, Comparison

PASSING over what is said in this place about the validity
of inference, because we shall have to return to it hereafter,
we find Gotama bent on establishing by the side of it, by
the side of Anumana, his next instrument of knowledge,
namely Upamana, analogy or comparison. And here Gotama
seems in conflict with Kanada who, as we shall see, declines
to accept Upamana, comparison, as one of the independent
authoritative evidences, or, at all events, as essentially
different from Anumana, inference. We might feel tempted
to conclude from this that Gotama must have been later in
time than Kanada. But first of all, Kanada's name is not
mentioned here nor that of his system, Vaiseshika; and
secondly, we know that this question of the Pramanas had
been discussed again and again in every school of Indian
philosophy, so that a mere reference to the subject cannot
be used as determining the seniority either of the opponent
or of the defender. All we can say is that, whenever we
see Upamana appealed to as a means of valid knowledge,
we know that we have to deal with followers of the Nyaya
school; but the Vaiseshika, though denying it an independent place among the Pramanas, would by no means reject
it, if presented as a kind of Anumana.

Sabda, the Word

WE now come to the various kinds of verbal testimony.
Testimony is said to be conveyed by words, and by a sen-

tence, consisting of many words, conveying the meaning of each word in its relation to the other words. Though the meaning of words is admitted to be conventional, yet opinions differ because some consider such conventions to be eternal or divine, while others take them to be non-eternal or human. The chief authority for determining the meaning of a word is admitted to be the usage of trustworthy persons, but it is argued that as the highest authority is Brahman or God, and as the Veda is the word of Brahman, it follows that every word of the Veda possesses the highest authority. This, however, as we know, does not satisfy the Mimamsakas, who assign eternity to the Sabda itself, the word or the sound of a word.

In the examination of the validity of Sabda or word, we find again the same question started as before, whether it deserves a place by itself, or whether it should not rather be treated as a kind of inference. Then, after Gotama has shown the difference between 'I know' and 'I infer,' between acceptance of the word of an authority (Apto-padesa) and reliance on an inference, he enters on new problems such as the association of sense with sound, a question which is intimately connected with the question of what authority is due to the Veda as the Word *par excellence*. Here we meet with a number of arguments in defence of the supreme authority of the Veda with which we are familiar from the Purva-Mimamsa, but which again, though clearly referring to Jaimini, must not be taken to prove the anteriority of Jaimini's Sutras to those of Gotama's, and certainly do not enable us to admit more than the contemporaneous activity of the various schools of Hindu philosophy during the centuries intervening be-tween the close of the Vedic age and the rise and spread of Buddhism.

The Eight Pramanas

HAVING defended the teaching of the Nyaya, that there are four Pramanas, neither more nor less, Gotama proceeds to criticise the four additional Pramanas of the Mimam-sakas, and shows that their number is superabundant. They include, as we saw, Aitihya, tradition, not necessarily authoritative, Arthapatti, assumption, Sambhava, probabi-

lity; and even Abhava, non-existence, because they hold
that there can be knowledge arising from not-being or,
from absence, as when we conclude from the fact that
Devadatta is not in his house, that he must have gone out.
Of these four Pramanas the first is referred by Gotama to
Sabda, Word, the others to Anumana, inference, while
Cheshta, or mere gesture, as supplying knowledge, may, it
is added, be classed either under Word, like written letters,
or under Anumana. The Pramanas seem to have formed
a subject of prominent interest to the Nyaya philosophers;
in modern times they have absorbed the whole of Nyaya.
We are told that Nagarjuna, before he became a Buddhist,
was a zealous student of the Nyaya-philosophy. He wrote
a work, called Pramana-samuchchaya, which was, however,
supposed to be lost, till Sarat Chandra discovered a Tibetan
version of it in the library of the Grand Lama at Lhassa
(Journal of the Buddhist Text Society, IV, parts iii and
iv, p. 17)[1].

Here follow long discussions as to the nature of words,
the difference between sound (Dhvani) and words, till we
arrive again at the question whether the word is eternal,
and therefore a Pramana by itself, or not. Similar questions occur in most of the Indian philosophical systems,
and as I passed them over before, it will be necessary to
examine them more fully in this place, where we meet with
them again as worked out by Gotama. Though they deal
with such purely grammatical questions as whether a vowel
such as i can ever be changed into the semi-vowel y, in
fact whether any letter can ever become another letter,
these disquisitions branch out very far, and we shall be
surprised to see how intimately in the minds of Hindu
philosophers they are connected with some of the greatest
problems of philosophy, such as the existence of a Creator
and the relation between the cause and the effect of our
created world.
The oftener we read these discussions on the eternal
character of sound, on words and their true nature, and at
last on the divine, nay transcendental character of language.

[1] This would prove at the same time the study of the Nyaya
philosophy in the first century of our era.

the more we shall feel the difference between Eastern and Western philosophy. The true problem of language has been almost entirely neglected by Greek philosophers and their disciples in Europe, for all the discussions about the *phusei* or *thesei* origin of language touch only the very hem of the questions, as it presents itself to Indian philosophers. The way in which the problem of language is handled by them will no doubt be dismissed as childish by modern philosophers, and I do not mean to deny that some of their remarks on language are really childish. But we shall see that the whole question is treated by Hindu philosophers in a very serious and searching spirit. Students of philosophy should overlook what may seem strange to them in the manner of treatment, and always try to keep their eye on what is important and has often been overlooked even by the greatest thinkers among us. Language has been to most of us so familiar a subject that we have hardly perceived what is behind it, and have scarcely asked the questions which it has cost so much effort to Indian philosophers to answer. We have already on a former occasion examined some of the views on language, as expressed in the philosophical hymns, Brahmanas, and Upanishads of the Vedic period. We have now to follow up these views as they are presented to us in a more systematic form in the Sutra-period.

Thoughts on Language

IF I was right in tracing the word Brih, speech, in Brihas-pati, back to the same root as that of Brahman, the connection of the two ideas, Word and Creator, would carry us back even beyond what we call the Vedic period. At all events the idea that Brahman was the Word, and that the world was created by the Word, existed, as we saw, long before the rise of philosophical systems. It was shadowed forth in the very language of India, but it received its full development in the Sutras only, more particularly in the Vedanta-Sutras, to which we must return for our present purpose. We read in Sutra I, 3, 28: ' We refute his objection on the ground that (the world) originates from the Word, as is shown both by perception and by inference.' Perception is here taken in the sense of

Sruti; scripture, and inference in the sense of Smriti, tradition. An objection had been started that the Veda could not be considered as eternal, if it contained names of non-eternal things, and as even the gods, the Devas, were looked upon as non-eternal, having been proved to be subject to birth and rebirth, it followed that the Veda, as containing their names, could not possibly be ante-temporal or eternal. Against this, though readily admitting the non-eternal character of the gods, the Devas, Samkara argues, that in spite of that, the gods and other beings, nay the whole word, must be admitted to have originated from the Word or the Veda, and that this Word is Brahman. Only, he adds, it is not the individuals, nor this or that Deva, not this or that cow or horse, that had their origin in the Word, but the genus to which they belong, that is, the *eide* (Akritis). It is with the genus that words are connected, not with individuals, for these, as being infinite in number, are not capable of entering into that connection. Hence all individual things, and individual gods also, are allowed to have had an origin, but not the genus to which they belong, which was thought and uttered at first by Brahman. Nor must it be supposed that the Word constitutes the material cause of things; this, as shown before, lies in Brahman only, which is therefore more than the Word. The word of the Veda is simply the expression of what is permanent and eternal in all things (*universalia in rebus*), and as all individual things are created in accordance with it, they are rightly said to have their true origin in the Veda and in Brahman. This is afterwards confirmed by passages from Sruti and Smriti, such as Brih. Ar. Up. I, 2, 4: 'Then with his mind he united himself with Speech.' The Word therefore, or Speech, existed before creation, as we read in the Smriti also, *e.g.* the Mahabharata XII, 8534: 'He who exists by himself let first stream forth the Word, the eternal, without beginning or end, the Divine Word which we read in the Veda, whence proceeded the evolution of the world'; and again, Mahabh. XII, 8535: 'God in the beginning created the names and forms of things, and the continuous process of their works.'

If we read such passages carefully, it is easy to see that

Veda, which is identified with the words of creation, or the ideas or *logoi* of the world, was meant for more than what was afterwards called the three Vedas, the Samhitas, and Brahmanas. Veda stands here for *Logos* or *Sophia*, and comprehends all named concepts, necessary for the creation of all created things.

In order to show that there is nothing strange in this, Samkará remarks that even we ourselves, when we mean to do anything, have first to think of the word for what we mean to do. In the same manner the words of the Veda had to be present to the mind of the Creator, Prajapati, before he could have created the things corresponding to them. And thus it is said in the Veda (Taitt. Br. II, 2, 4, 2) : ' " This is the earth," he said, and created the earth.' This will sound strange to many readers, as, I confess, it sounded strange to me when I first came across these thoughts, so full of Neo-platonic reminiscences, nay even to such O. T. thought as ' God spake, Let there be light, and there was light.' Of course, if we can bring ourselves to say that the *Logos* of the Alexandrian philosophers had no antecedents in early Greek philosophy[1], there would be an end of the whole question, and we should simply have to admit that Brahmans came to Alexandria, and indoctrinated pagan and Christian philosophers with their ideas of Vach or Speech. But as every Greek scholar knows that the very opposite is the case, and I have tried to show this on several occasions, the question requires a very different solution from that proposed by Professor Weber, if indeed it admits of any. Why will people not see that it is far more scholarlike to confess our ignorance than to give an answer, however hesitatingly, and thus to discourage further research?

Hindu philosophers have treated this whole question with so much care that we can see at least that they truly cared for it, and had fully perceived its intimate connection with some of the highest problems, both religious and philosophical, which were nearest to their heart.

They begin with the beginning and try first to make it clear to themselves what Sabda is. Sabda means word,

[1] See Anathon Aall, *Geschichte der Logosidee*, 1896, pp. 218 seq.

but it also means sound, and they therefore begin with
asking what sound is. We have seen already that they
actually postulated a fifth element Akasa, which we translate by ether, and which was meant to be the vehicle of
sound and of sound only. The existence of this fifth
element was altogether denied by the materialists, the
Barhaspatyas, because it is supersensible, but it was
admitted as an independent element by the other schools
of thought, even by the Buddhists, because they held that
air could not possibly be the vehicle of sound. Its loud-
ness might depend on it, but not its quality. The Vaiseshika-philosophy, for instance, which takes a special interest
in the question of the elements, explains sound as the
object apprehended by the sense of hearing (II, 2, 21). It
then declares that sound is neither substance nor action,
but a quality (cf. I, 1, 6 com.); having Akasa or ether for
its substance. The opinion that sound exists always and
eternally, and is only made manifest by each speaker,
which is held by the Mimamsakas, is rejected by Kanada,
sounds and words being accepted as momentary manifestations only of eternal sound. This is illustrated by the
striking of a drum with a drumstick, where we can clearly
see that sound is produced by a conjunction between a
drum and a drumstick, and that it is only carried along by
the air.

All these arguments are clearly directed against the
Mimamsakas who for reasons of their own require Sabda,
whether sound or word, to be eternal. It must be said,
however, to their honour that they allow full credit to
the Purvapakshin who opposes the eternal character of
sounds and words. ' No,' he says[1], ' sound cannot be eternal,
because we see (1) that it is a product, (2) that it passes
away, (3) that it is made (the very letters being called
A-kara, Ka-kara &c., A-making, Ka-making &c.). We see
(4) that it is perceived by different persons at once, (5) that
it changes (as Dadhi Atra changes to Dadhy Atra), and
(6) that it is augmented by the number of those who make
it. But to all these difficulties the Mimamsaka has a ready

---

[1] Cf. Ballantyne's Mimamsa-Sutras, p. 8; Muir, Orig. Sansk. Texts,
III, pp. 70 seq.

answer. The word is eternal, he says, and though the perception of sound is the same on both sides, we are right in looking on sound as eternal and as always present, only not always manifested on account of the absence of an utterer or an exciter. The letter k, now heard, is the same which has always been heard. If it is said that sound is made, that only means that it is employed, and if it is perceived at the same time by many, the same applies to the sun. As to the modification of sound, it is not the same letter modified, but it is another letter in the place of a letter, and as to the increase of noise, that is due to the increase of the number of conjunctions and disjunctions of the air.

Jaimini's reasons in support of the eternal character of sound are that, though the sound may vanish, it leaves its traces in the mind of the hearer or learner; that it is everywhere at the same time; that, if repeated, it is the same, and that we have no right to suppose that it is ever annihilated. If it should be supposed that sound is a mere modification of air, the answer is that the ear does not simply hear the air, but is sensitive only to what is intangible in sound, the quality. Besides, there are the definite words of the Veda which tell us of an eternal Voice.

Having thus established to his own satisfaction the eternity of sound, Jaimini proceeds to defend the sounds or words of the Veda against all possible objections. These arguments were examined by us before, when the author-ship of the Veda had to be discussed, and when it was shown that the author of the Veda could not have been a personal being, but that the Veda could only have been seen by inspired Rishis as revealed to them, not as made by them. We may therefore at once proceed to the next point, namely, to the question, as to what constitutes a word, and what according to Indian philosophers is its real character. Though these discussions are of a grammatical rather than of a philosophical character, they deserve our attention, because they show how keen an interest the ancient philosophers of India had taken in the Science of Language, and how clearly they had perceived the intimate relation between language and thought, and in consequence between the Science of Language and the Science of Thought or Philosophy.

· How well the Hindus understood that the study of language forms an integral part of philosophy, we may gather from the fact that they actually admitted Panini, their greatest grammarian, among their representative philosophers. They had evidently perceived that language is the only phenomenal form of thought, and that, as human beings possess no means of perceiving the thoughts of others, nay even their own thoughts, except in the form of words, it was the duty of a student of thought to inquire into the nature of words before he approached or analysed the nature of what we mean by thought, naked thought, nay skinned thought, as it has been truly called, when divested of its natural integuments, the words. They understood what even modern philosophers have failed to understand, that there is a difference between *Vorstellung* (presentation or percept) and *Begriff* (concept), and that true thought has to do with conceptual words only, nay that the two, word and thought, are inseparable, and perish when separated. Madhava in his survey of all philosophies, assigns a place between Jaimini's Purva-Mimamsa and Kapila's Samkhya to the Panini Darsana, what we should call the grammatical system of Panini. Other systems also treat most fully of linguistic questions, as, for instance, the Purva-Mimamsa when treating of the question whether sound, the material element of words, is eternal or not.

Sphota

HINDU philosophers have actually elaborated an idea which does not exist in any other philosophy, that of Sphota. It is true that in Panini's own Sutras the word Sphota does not occur, but the name of a grammarian whom he quotes (VI, 1, 123), Sphotayana, shows that this peculiar word Sphota must have existed before Panini's time. Derived as it is from Sphut, Sphota must have meant originally what bursts forth. It has been translated by expression, notion, concept or idea, but none of these renderings can be considered as successful. It really means the sound of a word as a whole, and as conveying a meaning, apart from its component letters. The subject has been well treated by Madhava in his Sarva-darsana-samgraha. Here, when examining the Panini Darsana, he shows first of all that the Sabda or word which Panini professes to teach in his Sabdanusasana, or grammar, is really the same as Brahman. 'The eternal word,' he writes, 'which is called Sphota, and is without parts, is the true cause of the world,' is in fact Brahman, and he adds thereupon some lines from Bhartrihari's Brahmakanda, where that grammarian (died 650 A.D.) says:—

Brahman, without beginning or end, the indestructible essence of language,
Which developed in the form of things, and whence springs the creation of the world.'

What more could be said of the Neo-platonic Logos?

In answer to some who deny the existence of such a Sphota, it is maintained that it is actually an object of perception, for all men, on hearing the word 'cow,' know it as distinct from the letters composing it. This shows, as we knew already from the Pratisakhyas, that the Hindus had elaborated the idea of letters, nay even of vowels and consonants, long before they became acquainted with the written letters of a Semitic alphabet, and I only wonder that those who believe in an ancient indigenous alphabet, should never have appealed, though vainly, to the discussions of Sphota, in support of their opinion. And if it were said that cognition arises from the separate letters of a word, we ask, he says, whether these letters are supposed to produce cognition in their collective or in their separate form. It cannot be in their collective form, because each letter, as soon as pronounced, vanishes, and therefore cannot form a whole; nor can it be in their separate form, because no single letter has the power of producing cognition of the meaning of any word. As therefore the letters, whether in their single or their united form, cannot produce cognition, there must be something else by means of which knowledge is produced, and that is the Sphota, the sound, distinct from the letters though revealed by them. He then quotes from Patanjali's Maha-bhashya: 'Now what is the word Cow? It is that by which, when pronounced, there is produced in us the simultaneous cognition of dewlap, tail, hump, hoofs, and horns.'

Kaiyata explains this more fully by saying: 'Grammarian's maintain that it is the word, as distinct from the letters, which expresses the meaning, since, if the letters expressed it, there would be no use in pronouncing the second and following ones (as the first would already have conveyed all that is wished). It is therefore something distinct from the single letters which conveys the meaning, and that is what we call the Sphota.'

The objector, however, is not silenced at once. He, too, asks the question whether this Sphota is manifest or non-manifest. If it required no manifestation, it would always be there, but if it requires manifestation, this could be by its letters only, when they are pronounced; and thus the same difficulties which were pointed out before as to the collective or single action of letters, would arise again. This dilemma is put forward by Bhatta in his Mimamsa-sloka-varttika: 'The grammarian who holds that Sphota is manifested by the letters as they are severally pronounced and apprehended, though itself one and indivisible, does not thereby escape from a single difficulty.'

On this point Panini (I, 4, 14,) seems to have given the right solution, by laying it down as a principle that letters can never form a word unless they have an affix at the end, while the letters, as they are apprehended, simply help to convey the meaning by means of a conventional association (*thesei*). This shows that the conventional character of the relation between sound and meaning was fully recognised in India, whether that sound was called Sabda or Sphota. Nor is it enough that the letters should be the same, they must also follow each other in the same order, otherwise Vasa and Sava, Nava and Vana, &c., would carry the same meaning, which they do not.

All this was meant to show that the admission of a Sphota was unnecessary; but we now get the orthodox answer, namely, that the admission of Sphota is necessary, and that all the objections are no more than a catching at a straw by a drowning person, because separate letters would never be a word, as little as flowers without a string would be a wreath. And as the letters cannot combine, being evanescent as soon as they have been pronounced,

we are asked to admit a Sphota, and to accept the first
letters, as revealing the invisible Sphota, whereas the
following letters serve only to make that Sphota more and
more manifest and explicit.

Words express the *Summum Genus*

AFTER having thus in his own way established the theory
of a Sphota for every word, our philosophical grammarian
takes another step, trying to prove that the meaning of all
words is ultimately that *summum genus* (Satta), namely
pure existence, the characteristic of which is consciousness
of the supreme reality.   And lest it should be thought
that in that case all words would mean one and the same
thing, namely Brahman or being, it is remarked that in one
sense this is really so; but that, as a crystal is coloured by
its surroundings, Brahman, when connected with different
things and severally identified with each, stands afterwards for different species, such as cow, horse, &c., these
being first of all 'existence' (Satta) or the highest genus,
as found in individuals, and then only what they are in
this phenomenal world.   In support of this another passage
of Bhartrihari's is quoted: 'Existence being divided, as
found in cows, &c., is called this or that species by means
of its connection with different objects, and on it all words
depend.   This they call the meaning of the stem, and the
meaning of the root.   This is existence, this is the great
Atman (or Brahman), expressed by affixes such as Tva, Tal,
&c., which form abstract nouns, such as Go-tva, cow-hood,
&c.   For existence, as the *summum genus*, is found in all
things, in cows, horses, &c., and therefore all words, expressive of definite meanings, rest ultimately on the *summum
genus*, existence, differentiated by various thoughts or words,
such as cows, horses, &c., in which it resides.   If the stem-
word, the Pratipadika, expresses existence, the root expresses Bhava, a state, or, as others say, Kriya, action.'
    This will remind us of many of the speculations of Greek
as well as medieval logicians; and it is exactly what my
late friend Noire tried to establish, that all words originally
expressed action, to which I added the amendment that
they expressed either an action or a status.   If this true
kernel of every word is by Hindu philosophers called the

Great Atman (Mahan Atma), and Satta, the *summum genus*, we must remember that, according to the Vedanta, Brahman is the true substance of everything. This is stated again by Bhartrihari:

'The true reality is known under its illusory forms, by words under untrue disguises; the true reality is named (for a time), like the house of Devadatta, so called for a vanishing reason (that, is, only so long as Devadatta is the possessor of the house); but by the word house, pure household[1] only is expressed.'

Words expressive of Genera or Individuals?

BUT while the meaning of all words is thus admitted to be Brahman, we meet with two schools, the one of Vajapyayana, maintaining that our ordinary words mean a genus, the other, of Vyadi, who holds that they mean individual things. Panini holds both views as true in grammar, for in one place, I, 2, 58, he shows that 'a Brahman' may mean many Brahmans, as when we say, that a Brahman is to be honoured; in another, I, 2, 64, he states that the plural Ramas means always Rama, Rama and Rama, i.e. so many single Ramas.

All Words mean *to on*

THE idea that all words in the end mean Brahman, the one Supreme Being, was necessitated by the very character of the Vedanta-philosophy, which admits of no duality except as the result of nescience. Hence it is said: The Supreme Being is the thing denoted by all words, and it is identical with the word; but the relation of the two, while they are ultimately identical, varies as it does in the case of the two Atmans, the Paramatman and the Jivatman, the highest or universal, and the living or individual soul, the difference between the two being due to Avidya or temporary nescience. As early as the Maitrayana Upanishad we meet with verses to the same effect, and of an earlier date than itself, such as (VI, 22), 'Two Brahmans have to be meditated on, the Word and the Non-word, and

---

[1] Read Grihatvam instead of Grihitam?

by the Word alone is the Non-word revealed.' In this way the grammatical philosophers endeavoured to prove that grammar or exposition of words, as it was called by Patanjali (Sabdanusasana), is, like every other system of philosophy, 'the means of final beatitude, the door of emancipation, the medicine of the diseases of language, the purifier of all sciences, the science of sciences ; it is the first rung on the ladder that leads up to final bliss, and the straight royal road among all the roads that lead to emancipaton.'

This may be accepted as representing the views, if not of Panini himself, at least of his followers; and I must say that if his explanation of a word as a number of letters ending in a suffix had been accepted, there would have been no necessity for the admission of a Sphota. It was evidently not seen by the inventors of this Sphota that letters have no independent existence at all, and can be considered only as the result of a scientific analysis, and that words existed long before even the idea of letters had been formed. Letters, by themselves, have no *raison d'etre*. Sphota is in fact the word before it had been analysed into letters, the breaking forth of a whole and undivided utterance, such as Go, 'cow,' conveying a meaning which does not depend on any single letter nor on any combination of them. Though from our point of view the idea of such a Sphota may seem unnecessary, we cannot help admiring the ingenuity of the ancient philosophers of India in inventing such a term, and in seeing difficulties which never attracted the attention of European philosophers. For it is perfectly true that the letters, as such, have no reality and no power, and that every word is something different from its letters, something undivided and indivisible. In such a word as *Vak*, Vox, we have not a combination of three letters, v, a, *k*, which would be nothing, but we have an indivisible explosion, expressive of its meaning in its undivided form only, and this may be raised to the status of a word by means of a grammatical suffix which, as we should say, makes an organised whole of it. All this is true and recognised now by all students of the Science of Language, though never even suspected by the philosophers of other countries.

Still more important is the idea that all words originally meant Brahman or *to on*, and receive their special meaning from their relation to the genera or *logoi* in the mind of Brahman, as creative types. Words are not names of individuals, but always of classes or genera, and as genera they are eternal. These *logoi* existed before the creation of the world, nay, rendered that creation possible. This is the much-despised Neo-platonic philosophy, the basis of the Christian theory of creation; and that we should find it so fully elaborated in the ancient world of India is surely a surprise, and, I should add, a welcome surprise. And can we suppose that ideas which, in Greece, required so many evolutions of thought till they reached the point which they reached in Alexandria, and afterwards in Palestine, should have sprung up in India suddenly or, as it were, casually? Do we not rather see clearly here also how long and how continuous a development of thought must have taken place south of the Himalayas before such fruits could have ripened? Would any Greek scholar dare to say that all this was borrowed from Greece? Would any Sanskrit scholar be so intrepid as to hint that the Greeks might possibly have learnt their *Logos* from the Vedic Vach? Even if we do not accept the last results of this Indian line of thought, which ended where Greek philosophy ended, and where Christian philosophy began, nay even if we should put aside as unintelligible the beginning words of the fourth Gospel, 'In the beginning was the Word,' we can at least admire the struggle which led up to this view of the world, and tried to establish the truth that there is a *Logos*, thought, that there is Rhyme and Reason in the world, and that the whole universe is full of Brahman, the Eternal and the Divine, not visible to the human eye, though visible to the human mind. That mind, according to Indian philosophy, has its true being in the Divine Mind, in which it lives and moves, in which alone it has its true Self or Atman, which Atman is Brahman. To have mounted to such heights, even if we have to descend again frightened and giddy, must have strengthened the muscles of human reason, and will remain in our memory as a sight never to be forgotten, even in the lower spheres in which we have to move in our daily life and amidst our daily duties. Speaking for myself, I am bound to say that I have felt an acquaintance with the general spirit of Indian philosophy as a blessing from my very youth, being strengthened by it against all the antinomies of being and thinking, and nerved in all the encounters with the scepticism and materialism of our own ephemeral philosophy. It is easy, no doubt, to discover blemishes in the form and style of Indian philosophy, I mean chiefly the Vedanta, and to cite expressions which at first sight seem absurd. But there are such blemishes and such absurdities in all philosophies, even in the most modern. Many people have smiled at the Platonic ideas, at the atoms of Democritus, or at the location of the soul in the pineal gland or in certain parts of the brain; yet all this belongs to the history of philosophy, and had its right place in it at the right time. What the historian of philosophy has to do is first of all to try to understand the thoughts of great philosophers, then to winnow what is permanent from what is temporary, and to discover, if possible, the vein of gold that runs through the quartz, to keep the gold, and to sweep away the rubbish. Why not do the same for Indian philosophy? Why not try to bring it near to us, however far removed from it we may seem at first sight? In all other countries philosophy has railed at religion and religion has railed at philosophy. In India alone the two have always worked together harmoniously, religion deriving its freedom from philosophy, philosophy gaining its spirituality from religion. Is not that something to make us think, and to remind us of the often-repeated words of Terence, *Humani nihil a me alienum puto*? A rich kernel is often covered by a rough skin, and true wisdom may be hiding where we least expect it.

Vedanta on Sphota

WE have now to see what the other systems of philosophy have to say on this subject, for it is quite clear that the idea of a Sphota, though known to them, was not accepted by all. Samkara, as representing the Vedanta-philosophy, is entirely opposed to the admission of a Sphota. He fully admits that earth and all the rest were created according to the words earth, &c., which were present to

the mind of the Creator, but he asks, how were these words
present? Beginning as usual with the Purvapakshin[1] or
opponent, he produces as arguments in favour of the admission of a Sphota, that the letters cannot convey the meaning,
because as soon as they are pronounced they perish, because
they differ according to the pronunciation of each speaker,
because they possess neither singly nor collectively any
significative power, because not even the last letter with
the impression left by the preceding letter in our memory,
would convey to us the sense of a word. Hence something
different from the letters must be admitted, the Sphota, the
outburst of the whole word, presenting itself all at once as
the object of our mental act of apprehension. That Sphota
is what is eternal, different therefore from perishable and
changeable letters, and it is that Sphota from which whatever is denoted by it was produced in creation, and which
in conversation conveys to others what is in our own mind,
but always clothed in sound.

Samkara himself, however, considers such an admission
of a Sphota entirely unnecessary, and, in order to prove
this, he goes back and calls to his aid an old Vedantist,
Upavarsha, whom he refers to elsewhere also (III, 3, 53)[2].
This Upavarsha argues that the letters by themselves con-
stitute the word, because though they perish as fast as they
are pronounced, they are always recognised again as the
same letters, not only as belonging to the same class, but
as actually the same. Thus when the word cow is pronounced twice, we do not think that two words have been
pronounced, but that the same word has been pronounced
twice. And though two individuals may, no doubt, pro-
nounce the same word differently, such differences are due
to the organs of pronunciation, and not to the intrinsic
nature of the letters. He holds that the apprehension of
difference depends on external factors, but that their recognition is due only to the intrinsic nature of the letters. The

[1] Ved. Sutras 1, 3, 28. This is one of the cases where the Purvapaksha, the opponent's view, has been mistaken for Samkara's own
final opinion, or for the Siddhanta.

[2] Here Samkara charges Sabarasvamin, the famous commentator
on the Purva-Mimamsa, 1, 1, 5, with having borrowed an argument
from Badarayana.

sound which enters the ear (Dhvani) may be different, strong or weak, high or low, but the letters through all this are recognised as the same. And if it be said that the letters of a word, being several, cannot form the object of one mental act, this is not so, because the ideas which we have of a row, or a wood, or an army, show that things which comprise several unities can become objects of one and the same act of cognition. And if it be asked why groups of letters such as Pika and Kapi should convey different meanings, viz. cuckoo and ape, we have only to look at a number of ants, which as long as they move one after another in a certain order, convey the idea of a row, but cease to do so if they are scattered about at random.

Without adducing further arguments, Samkara in the end maintains that the admission of a Sphota is unnecessary, and that it is simpler to accept the letters of a word as having entered into a permanent connection with a definite sense, and as always presenting themselves in a definite order to our understanding, which, after apprehending the several letters, finally comprehends the entire aggregate as conveying a definite sense. We never perceive a Sphota, he argues, and if the letters are supposed to manifest the Sphota, the Sphota in turn would have to manifest the sense. It would even be preferable to admit that letters form a genus, and as such are eternal, but in either case we should gain nothing by the Sphota that we could not have without it, by the admission of eternal words from which all non-eternal things, such as gods, cows, and horses, originated. Hence we see that, though the theory of the Sphota is rejected by the Vedanta, the eternal character of the words is strenuously retained, being considered essential, as it would seem, in order to maintain the identity of Brahman and the Word, and the creation of the world by Brahman in accordance with the eternal words.

Yoga and Samkhya on Sphota

THE Yoga-philosophy accepted the theory of the Sphota, nay it has been supposed to have first originated it[1], for, according to the commentary, it was against the Yoga

---

[1] Garbe, Samkhya-Philosophie, p. 111 n.

philosophers, rather than against the Mimamsa, that
Kapila's objections concerning the Sphota were directed.
What Kapila says about Sphota is of much the same character as what he had said about Isvara, the Lord, namely that
its existence cannot be proved, not that it does not exist.
If Sphota, he says, is meant for the group of letters forming
a word, then why not be satisfied with this, and simply
speak of a word (Pada), as manifesting its sense? Why
invent something which has never been perceived, and
which exists as little apart from the letters as a forest exists
apart from the trees, what is in fact entirely gratuitous
(V, 57)?

Nor are the letters, from Kapila's point of view, eternal
(V, 58), because, as Badarayana also remarked, we can wit-
ness their production; and our being able to recognise them
as the same, proves no more than their belonging to one and
the same genus, but not their being eternal.

It is curious to observe the elaborateness with which
what seems to us a purely grammatical question is discussed in the various schools of Indian philosophy. The
Sphota, however, is to Indian thinkers not merely a grammatical problem; it is distantly connected with the question
of the eternity of the Veda. This eternity is denied by
Kapila (Samkhya V, 46) because the Vedas speak of themselves as having been produced in such passages as: ' He
became heated, and from him, thus heated, the three Vedas
were produced.' Eternity of the Veda can therefore, according to Kapila, mean no more than an unbeginning and
unbroken continuity, so that even at the beginning of a new
creation the order of words in the Veda remains the same
as before. But if, as Nyaya and Vaiseshika maintain, this
Veda was the work of a personal being, such as Isvara, this
is declared impossible by Kapila, because, as he holds, such
an Isvara has never been proved to exist. For he holds that
the Lord or Isvara could only have been either a liberated
or an unliberated Purusha. Now a liberated Purusha, such
as Vishnu for instance, could not have composed this enor-
mous Veda, because he is free from all desires, nor could an
active, non-liberated Purusha have been the author, because
he would not have possessed the omniscience required for
such a work.

But we must not conclude that, because we know of no possible personal author, therefore the Veda is eternal, in the same way as germs and sprouts. What is called the work of a personal being always presupposes a corporeal person, and it presupposes a will. We should not call the mere breathing of a person in sleep, a personal work. But the Vedas, as we read, rise spontaneously like an exhalation from the Highest Being, not by any effort of will, but by some miraculous virtue. It must not be supposed that the words of the Veda are manifested, like the notes of birds, without any purpose or meaning. No, they are the means of right knowledge, and their innate power is proved by the wonderful effects which are produced, for instance, by medical formulas taken from the Ayur-veda. This is the same argument which was used in the Nyaya-Sutras II, 68, as a tangible and irrefutable proof of the efficiency of the Vedas. Here all would depend on the experimental proof, and this the Hindus, ancient or modern, would find it difficult to supply ; but if the Hindus were satisfied, we have no reason to find fault.

Nyaya on Sphota

If now we turn to the Nyaya-philosophy we find that Gotama also denies the eternity of sound, because, it is argued, we can see that it has a beginning or cause, because it is an object of sense-perception, and because it is known to be factitious. Besides, if sound were eternal, we should be able to perceive it always, even before it is uttered, there being no known barrier between the ether and our ear (II, 3, 86). This ethereal substratum of sound is, no doubt, intangible (II, 3, 104), but it is nevertheless a something perceptible by one of our senses, that of hearing, and hence it must be non-eternal. The true eternity of the Vedas consists, according to Gotama, in the unbroken continuity of their tradition, study and employment, both in the Man-vantaras and Yugas which are past and those that are still to come, whilst their authority depends on the authority of the most competent persons. This is the same with secular words[1]. This last admission would of course be strongly

---

[1] Vatsyayana's Commentary on the Nyaya, p. 91, ed. Biblioth. Indica, Muir, O. S. T., III, p. 115.

7252

resisted and resented by Vedanta philosophers, but it shows at all events the freedom with which all Indian philosophers were allowed to handle the ancient Sacred Books of the country.

Vaiseshika on Sphota

The Vaiseshikas lastly do not differ much from the Naiyayikas as to whether the Veda is eternal or not, is authoritative or not, but they follow their own way of reasoning. The very last Sutra of the Vaiseshika-Sastra, X, 2, 9, says : ' It has been declared that authoritativeness belongs to the Amnaya (Veda) because it is uttered by Him '; and this declaration is found likewise in the third Sutra of the first book to which the final Sutra refers. But though this Sutra is given twice, there attaches some uncertainty to its meaning, because, as pointed out by the Indian commentators, the words ' because uttered by Him,' may also be translated by ' because it declares it,' i.e., ' because it teaches duty (Dharma).' But in either case there are objections, the same as those with which we are familiar from the Purvapaksha in the Vedanta and Mimamsaka-Sutras, such as self-contradictoriness, tautology, and the rest discovered by some critics in the text of the Vedas. Thereupon the eternal character, too, of the Veda is called in question, and whoever its author may have been, whether human or divine, it is doubted whether he can justly claim any authority.

In answer to this sweeping condemnation the Vaiseshika points out VI, 1, 1, ' that at all events there is in the Veda a construction of sentences consequent upon intelligence,' or as we should say, the Veda must at least be admitted to be the work of a rational author, and not of an author of limited intelligence, because no merely rational author could propound such a rule as ' He who desires paradise, should sacrifice.' Such matters could not be known in their causes and effects to men of limited knowledge like ourselves. Whatever we may think of this argument, it shows at all events the state of mind of the earliest defenders of revelation. They argued that, because the author must at least be admitted to have been a rational being, he could not possibly have declared things that are beyond the knowledge of ordinary rational beings, such as the rewards of sacrifices in another world, and other matters beyond the ken of experience. The Vaiseshikas admitted a personal author of the Veda, an Isvara, but this by no means involved the eternity of the Veda. With the Vaiseshikas also, the eternity of the Veda meant no more than its uninterrupted tradition (Sampradaya), but some further supports to its authority were found in the fact that, besides being the work of a rational being, in this case of Isvara, the Lord, it had been accepted as the highest authority by a long line of the great or greatest men who themselves might safely be regarded, if not as infallible, at least as trustworthy and authoritative.

Prameyas, Objects of Knowledge

If now, after an examination of the various opinions entertained by the Nyaya and other Hindu philosophers of the significative power of words, we return to the Sutras of Gotama, we find that, in his third book, he is chiefly concerned with the Prameyas, that is, the objects of knowledge, as established by the Pramanas ; and the first question that meets us is whether the senses or Indriyas, the instruments of objective knowledge, should be treated as different from the Atman, the Self, or not.

Indriyas, Senses.

Gotama holds that they are different from the Atman ; and in order to prove this, he argues, that if each sense could perceive by itself, each sense would perceive its own object only, the ear sound, the eye colour, the skin warmth, &c.; and that therefore what perceives all these impressions together, at the same time and in the same object, must be something different from the several senses, namely the Atman, or, according to other systems, the Manas or mind.

Sarira, Body

Next follows the question whether the body is the same as the Atman, a question which would never occur to a Vedantist. But Gotama asks it and solves it in his own way. It cannot be, he says, because, when the body has once been destroyed by being burnt, the consequences of good and evil deeds would cease to pursue the Self through an endless series of births and rebirths. A number of similar objections and answers follow, all showing how much this question had occupied the thoughts of the Nyaya philosophers. Some of them suggest difficulties which betray a very low state of philosophical reasoning, while other difficulties are such that even in our own time they have not ceased to perplex minute philosophers. We meet with the question why, with the dual organ of vision, there is no duality of perception ; why, if memory is supposed to be a quality or mode of the Self, mere remembrance of an acid substance can make our mouth water. After these questions have been, if not solved, at least carefully considered, Gotama goes on to show that if the body be not Atman, neither can Manas, mind, be conceived as the Atman.

Manas, Mind

The Self is the knower, while the mind or Manas is only the instrument (Karana) of knowledge by which attention is fixed on one thing at a time. The Self is eternal, not of this life only, without beginning and therefore without end. And here a curious argument is brought in, different from the usual Indian arguments in support of our previous existence, to show that our Self does not begin with our birth on earth, because, as he says, the smile of a new-born child can only arise from memory of a previous experience. While our modern psycho-physiologists would probably see in the smiles or the cries of a new-born child a reflex action of the muscles, our Indian objector declares that such movements are to be considered as no more than the opening and closing of a lotus-flower. And when this view has been silenced by the remark that a child does not consist of the five elements only, is not in fact, as we should say, a mere vegetable, a new argument of the same character is adduced, namely the child's readiness to suck, which can only be accounted for, they say, by the child having, in a former life acquired a desire for milk. When this again has been rejected as no argument, because we see that iron

also moves towards a magnet, Gotama answers once more
that a child cannot be treated like a piece of iron. And
when, as a last resource, desire in general, as manifested
by a child, is appealed to as showing a child's previous
existence, and when this also has once more been answered
by the remark that a child, like every other substance, must
be possessed of qualities, Gotama finally dismisses all these
objectors by maintaining that desires are not simply qualities,
but can arise from experience and previous impressions
(Samkalpa) only.

The consideration of the body and of the substances of
which it consists, whether of earth only, or ·of three
elements, earth, water and fire, or of four, earth, water,
fire and air, or of five, because it displays the qualities of
the five, is naturally of small interest in our time. The
final solution only deserves our attention, in so far as it
clearly shows that the Nyaya also recognised in some cases
the authority of the Veda as supreme, by stating that the
body is made of earth, and why? 'Srutipramanyat,' 'because
scripture says so.'

What follows, the discussion of sight or of the visual ray-
proceeding from the eye, and the question whether we
possess one general sense only, or many, may contain
curious suggestions for the psycho-physiologist; but there
is little of what we mean by really philosophic matter in it.
The qualities assigned to the objects of perception are not
very different from what they are supposed to be in the
other systems of philosophy, and they may be passed
by here all the more because they will have to be considered
more fully when we come to examine the Vaiseshika system.

More interesting is the discussion which occupies the rest
of the third book. It is chiefly concerned with the nature
of Self (Atman), the mind (Manas), the difference between
the two, and their relation to knowledge. Here we should
remember that, according to I, 15, Buddhi (understanding).
Upalabdhi (apprehension), and Jnana (knowledge) are used
synonymously. Though there are many manifestations of
Manas, such as memory, inference, verbal testimony, doubt,
imagination, dreaming cognition, guessing, feeling of
pleasure, desire, and all the rest, yet its distinguishing
feature, we are told, is what we should call attention, or as

Gotama explains it (I, 16), 'the preventing of knowledge arising altogether.' This is declared to be due to attention, and in many cases this would be the best rendering of Manas. Manas is therefore often called the doorkeeper, preventing sensations from rushing in promiscuously and all at once. If therefore we translate Manas by mind, we must always remember its technical meaning in Indian philosophy, and its being originally different from Buddhi, understanding, which might often be rendered by light or the internal light that changes dark and dull impressions into clear and bright sensations, perceptions, and knowledge in general, or by understanding, at least so far as it enables us to transform and understand the dull impressions of the senses.

The difference between the philosophical nomenclatures in English and Sanskrit for the Manas and its various functions is so great that a translation is almost impossible, and I am by no means satisfied with my own. It should also be remembered that the same Sanskrit term has often very different meanings in different systems of philosophy.
. The Buddhi of the Nyaya philosophers, for instance, is totally different from the Buddhi of the Samkhyas. Their Buddhi is eternal, while the Buddhi of Gotama is distinctly declared to be non-eternal. The Buddhi of the Samkhya is a cosmic principle independent of the Self, and meant to account for the existence of the light of reason in the whole universe; while in the Nyaya-philosophy it signifies the subjective activity of thought in the acquisition of knowledge, or in the lighting up and appropriating of the inert impressions received by the senses. This knowledge can come to an end and vanish by forgetfulness, while an eternal essence, like the Buddhi of the Samkhyas, though it may be ignored, can never be destroyed.

Atman

IN answering the question, What is knowledge, Gotama declares in this place quite clearly that real knowledge belongs to the Atman only, the Self or the soul. It cannot belong to the senses and their objects (Indriyartha), because knowledge abides even when the senses and what they perceive have been suppressed. Nor does knowledge belong to the Manas, which is but the instrument of knowledge, but it arises from the conjunction of Atman (Self) with Manas (attention), and on the other side of Manas with Indriyas (senses). Manas is the instrument, and the wielder of that instrument, like the wielder of an axe, must be some one different from it; this, according to the Nyaya, can only be the Self who in the end knows, who remembers, who feels pain and pleasure, who desires and acts.

Memory

MEMORY, Smriti, has not received from Indian philosophers the attention which it deserves. If it is treated as a means of knowledge, it falls under Anubhava, which is either immediate or mediate, and then called Smriti. Every Anubhava is supposed to leave an impression or modification of the mind, which is capable of being revived. There is another manifestation of memory in the act of remembering or recognising, as when on seeing a man we say, This is he, or This is Devadatta. Here we have Anubhava, knowledge of this, joined with something else, namely he or Devadatta, a revived Samskara, impression, or Smriti. The subject of memory is more fully treated in III, 113, and the various associations which awaken memory are enumerated as follows:

1. Attention to an object perceived;
2. Connection, as when the word Pramana, proof, recalls Prameya, what has to be proved;
3. Repetition, as when one has learned a number of things together, one calls up the other;
4. A sign, as when a thing recalls its *sine qua non;*
5. A mark, as when a standard reminds one of its bearer;
6. Likeness, as when one body recalls a similar body;
7. Possession, as when a property reminds us of its owner;
8. Belonging, when royal attendants remind us of the king;
9. Relation, as when a disciple reminds us of the teacher, or kine of a bull;
10. Succession, as when the pounding of rice reminds one of sprinkling;

11. Absence, as of a wife;
12. Fellow-workers, as when one disciple reminds us of the co-disciples;
13. Opposition, as when the ichneumon recalls the snake;
14. Pre-eminence, as when investiture with the sacred string recalls the principal agent, the Guru or teacher;
15. Receiving, as when a gift reminds one of the giver:
16. Covering, as when a sword reminds one of the sheath:
17. Pleasure and pain, each of which recalls the occasioner of it;
18. Desire and aversion, reminding us of their causes;
19. Fear, reminding us of what is feared, such as death;
20. Want, which makes us think of those who can supply our wants;
21. Motion, as when a shaking branch reminds us of the wind;
22. Affection, reminding us of a son, &c.;
23. Merit and Demerit, which make us reflect on joys and sorrows of a former life.

Such lists are very characteristic of Hindu philosophy, and they show at the same time that it is a mistake to ascribe them exclusively to the Samkhya-philosophy. Though they do not add much to our knowledge of the fundamental tenets of Indian philosophy, they show once more how much thought had been spent in the elaboration of mere details; and this, as we are told in this case by the commentator himself, chiefly in order to stir up the thoughts of the learners, Sishyavyutpadanaya, to independent activity.

Knowledge not Eternal

THE important point, however, which Gotama wishes to establish is this, that knowledge, though belonging to the eternal Self, is not in itself eternal, but vanishes like any other act. He also guards against the supposition that as we seem to take in more than one sensation at the same time, as in eating a cake full of different kinds of sweets, we ought to admit more than one Manas; and he explains that this simultaneousness of perception is apparent only, just as the fiery circle is when we whirl a firebrand with great rapidity, or as we imagine that a number of palm-leaves are pierced by a pin at one blow, and not in succession, one after the other. Lastly, he states that the Manas is Anu, infinitely small, or, as we should say, an atom.

More Prameyas

WHILE the third book was occupied with the first six of the Prameyas, or objects to be known and proved, including the whole apparatus of knowledge, such as Atman, Self or soul, Indriyas, senses, Manas, mind, central sensorium, Buddhi, understanding, and Sarira, body, and therefore gave rise to some important questions not only of metaphysics, but of psychology also, the fourth book which is devoted to the remaining six Prameyas, such as (7) Pravritti (activity), (8) Dosha (faults), (9) Pretyabhava (transmigration), (10) Phala (rewards), (11) Duhkha (pain), and (12) Apavarga (final beatitude), is naturally of a more practical character, and less attractive to the student of the problems of being and thinking. Some questions, however, are treated in it which cannot well be passed over, if we wish to give a full insight into the whole character, and the practical bearing of the Nyaya-philosophy.

Though this philosophy is supposed to represent Indian logic only, we have already seen enough of it to know that it included almost every question within the sphere of philosophy and religion, and that its chief object was the same as that of all the other systems of Indian philosophy, namely salvation.

Life after Death

ONE of the seven interesting subjects treated here is Pretyabhava, literally existence after having departed this life, and this is proved in a very short way. As the Self has been proved to be eternal, Gotama says (IV, 10) it follows that it will exist after what is called death. Some of the objections made to this tenet are easily disposed of, but nothing is said to establish what is meant by trans-migration, that is being born again in another world as either a human or as some other animal being, or even as a plant.

Existence of Deity

ANOTHER important subject, if it is not passed over alto-gether, is treated by Gotama, as it was by Kapila, inci-dentally only, I mean the existence of a Deity. It comes in when a problem of the Buddhists is under discussion, namely, whether the world came out of nothing, and whether the manifestation of anything presupposes the destruction of its cause. This is illustrated by the fact that the seed has to perish before the flower can appear. But Gotama strongly denies this, and reminds the opponent that if the seed were really destroyed by being pounded or burnt, the flower would never appear. Nor could it be said that the flower, if it had not existed previously, destroyed the seed, while, if it had, it would have owed its existence to the simple destruction of the seed. Therefore, he continues, as nothing can be produced from nothing, nor from an annihilated something, like a seed, the world also cannot have sprung from nothingness, but requires the admission of an Isvara, the Lord, as its real cause. And this admission of an Isvara, even though in the capacity of a governor rather than of a maker of the world, is con-firmed by what was evidently considered by Gotama as a firmly established truth, namely, that every act of man invariably produces its result, though not by itself, but under the superintendence of some one, that is, of Isvara. We then meet with a new argument, different from that of the Mimamsakas, namely that, if work done continued to work entirely by itself, the fact that some good or evil deeds of men do not seem to receive their reward would remain unaccounted for. This is certainly a curious way of proving the existence of God by the very argument which has generally been employed by those who want to prove His non-existence. Gotama's real object, however, is to refute the Buddhist theory of vacuity (Sunya), or of Nothing being the cause of the world, and afterwards to disprove the idea that effects can ever be fortuitous. And as Gotama differs from Gautama in denying the origin of the world out of nothing, he also differs from the Samkhya philosophers, who hold that all things, as developed out of Prakriti, are real only so long as they are noticed by the Purusha. He holds, on the contrary, that some things are real and eternal, but others are not, because we actually see both their production and their destruction. If we were to doubt this, we should doubt what has been settled by the authority of all men, and there would be an end of all truth and untruth. This[1] is a novel kind of argument for an Indian philosopher to use, and shows that with all the boldness of their speculations they were not so entirely different from ourselves, and not entirely indifferent to the *Securus judicat orbis terrarum.*

Cause and Effect

If, however, we call the Nyaya-philosophy theistic, we should always remember that such terms as theistic and atheistic are hardly applicable to Indian philosophy in the sense in which they are used by Christian theologians. With us atheistic implies the denial of a supreme and absolute Being; but we saw that even the so-called atheism of the Samkhya-philosophy does not amount to that. It is simply the denial of an Isvara, as an active and personal creator and ruler of the world.

And even such a personal God is not altogether denied by the Samkhyas; they only deny that He can be proved to exist by human arguments, and if He exists as such, they hold that in the eyes of philosophers He would be but a phenomenal manifestation of the Godhead, liable to change, liable even to temporary disappearance at the end of each aeon, and to reappearance at the beginning of a new aeon. It is this kind of a divine being, a personal Isvara or Lord, that is taken for granted by the Nyaya philosophers, and, it may be added at once, by the Vaiseshika philosophers also.[2]

In the Tarka-Samkraha, for instance, it is distinctly stated that 'the Atman or Self is twofold, the Jivatman (personal Self), and the Paramatman (the Highest Self).'

---

[1] Sarvalaukikapramatva.

[2] Ballantyne, Christianity contrasted with Hindu Philosophy, p. 12 ; Muir, O. S. T., vol iii, p. 133.

It must not be supposed, however, that Isvara, the omniscient Lord, is Pramatman, which is one only, while the Jivatman is separate for each individual body, all-pervading and eternal. Though Paramatman is Isvara, Isvara is not Paramatman, but a phenomenal manifestation of Paramatman only. The argument which we met with before is fully stated in Gotama's Sutras, IV, 19-21. The actions of men, it is said, do not always produce an effect. Good actions do not always produce good results, nor bad actions bad results, as they ought, if every act continued to act (Karman). Hence there must be another power that modifies the continuous acting of acts, and that can be Isvara only. It is not denied thereby that human actions are required, and that no effects would take place without the working of human agents, only they are not the sole cause of what happens, but we require another power, an Isvara, to account for what would otherwise be irrational results of human actions.

Phala, Rewards

WE now come to the tenth of the Prameyas, Phala; and here the same subject is treated once more, though from a different point of view. It is asked, how are effects, rewards or punishments, possible in another life? As both good and evil works are done in this life, the cause, namely these works, would have ceased to exist long before their fruit is to be gathered. This objection is met by an illustration taken from a tree which bears fruit long after it has ceased to be watered. The objector is not, however, satisfied with this, but, on the contrary, takes a bolder step, and denies that any effect either is or is not, at the same time. Gotama is not to be frightened by this apparently Buddhistic argument, but appeals again to what we should call the common-sense view of the matter, namely, that we actually see production and destruction before our very eyes. We can see every day that a cloth, before it has been woven, does not exist, for no weaver would say that the threads are the cloth, or the cloth the threads. And if it should be argued that the fruit produced by a tree is different from the fruit of our acts, because there is no receptacle (Asraya) or, as we should say, no subject, this is met by the declaration that, in the case of good or bad acts, there is a permanent receptacle, namely the Self, which alone is capable of perceiving pain or joy in this or in any other state of existence.

Emancipation

AFTER examining the meaning of pain, and expressing his conviction that everything, even pleasure, is full of pain, Gotama at last approaches the last subject, emancipation (Apavarga). He begins as usual with objections, such as that it is impossible in this life to pay all our moral debts, that certain sacrificial duties are enjoined as incumbent on us to the end of our lives, and that if it is said that a man is freed from these by old age, this does not imply that, even when he is no longer able to perform his daily duties, he should not perform certain duties, if in thought only. If, therefore, good works continue, there will be rewards for them, in fact there will be paradise, though even this would really have to be looked upon as an obstacle to real emancipation. Nothing remains but a complete extinction of all desires, and this can be effected by knowledge of the truth only. Therefore knowledge of the truth or removal of all false notions, is the beginning and end of all philosophy, and of the Nyaya-philosophy in particular. The first step towards this is the cessation of Ahamkara, here used in the sense of personal feelings, such as desire for a beautiful and aversion to a deformed object. Desire therefore has to be eradicated and aversion also; but before he explains how this desire, which arises from false apprehension (Mithyajnana) can be eradicated, Gotama is carried back once more to a subject which had been discussed before, namely whether the objects of desire exist as wholes or as parts. And this leads him on to what is the distinguishing doctrine both of the Nyaya and of the Vaiseshika-philosophies, namely the admission of Anus or atoms. If wholes are constantly divided and subdivided, we should in the end be landed in nihilism, but this is not to be. There cannot be annihilation because the Anus or the smallest parts are realities (IV, 8-82), and, according to their very nature, cannot be further reduced or compressed out of being. Against this view of the existence of what we should call atoms, the usual arguments are then adduced, namely that ether (or space) is everywhere, and therefore in an atom also, and if an atom has figure or a without and a within, it is of necessity divisible. In reply, ether is said to be intangible, neither resistant nor obstructing, that is, neither occupying space against others, nor preventing others from occupying space: and in the end an appeal is made to a recognised maxim of Hindu philosophy, that there must never be a *regressio in infinitum*, as there would be in attempting to divide an atom.

Knowledge of Ideas, not of Things

AND now the opponent, again, it would seem, a Buddhist, makes a still bolder sweep by denying the existence of any external things. All we have is knowledge, he says, not things; nothing different from our knowledge, or independent of our knowledge, can exist for us. Gotama objects to this (Vidyamatra) doctrine, first of all because, if it were impossible to prove the existence of any external things, it would be equally impossible to prove their non-existence. And if an appeal were made to dreams, or visions produced by a mirage, or by jugglery, it should be remembered that dreams also, like remembrances, presuppose previous perception of things; and that even in mistaking we mistake something, so that false knowledge can always be removed by true knowledge. After granting that, one more question arises, how that true knowledge, if once gained, is to be preserved, because we saw that knowledge is not eternal, but vanishes. And here the Nyaya suddenly calls the Yoga to its aid, and teaches that Samadhi or intense meditation will prove a safe preservative of knowledge, in spite of all disturbances from without, while the Nyaya-philosophy retains its own peculiar usefulness as employed in the defence of truth against all comers, in which case even such arts as wrangling and cavilling may prove of service.

This may seem a very humble view to take with regard to a system of philosophy which at the very outset promised to its students final beatitude as the highest reward. But considering the activity of philosophical speculation, of which we have had so many indications in the ancient as well as in the modern history of India, we can well understand that philosophers, skilled in all the arts and artifices of reasoning, would secure for their system that high position which the Nyaya certainly held and still holds[1] among the recognised systems of orthodox philosophy.   It would be useless to go once more over the topics from Jati, futility, No. XIV, to No. XVI, Nigrahasthana, objectionable proceedings, which are fully treated in the fifth book.

Syllogism

THERE is one subject, however, which requires some more special consideration, namely the Syllogism, or the Five Members, treated as VII.   This has always excited the special interest of European logicians on account of certain starting similarities which no doubt exist between it and the syllogism of Aristotle and the schoolman.   But from a Hindu point of view this syllogism or even logic in general is by no means the chief object of the Nyaya-philosophy, nor is it its exclusive property.   It has been fully discussed in the Vedanta and Samkhya systems, and once more in the Vaiseshika; but as it forms the pride of the Nyaya, it will find its most appropriate place here[2].

As we saw colour mentioned as the distinguishing quality of light, we found knowledge put forward as the characteristic feature of Self.   The Nyaya looks upon knowledge as inseparably connected with the Self, though in the larger sense of being the cause of every conception that has found expression in language.   Knowledge, according to the Nyaya, is either perception or remembrance.   Perception again is twofold, right or wrong.   Right perception represents a thing such as it is, silver as silver.   This is called truth, Prama.   Wrong perception represents a thing as it is not, mother-of-pearl as silver.

This right perception, according to the Nyaya-philosophy is, as we saw, of four kinds, sensuous, inferential, comparative, and authoritative, and is produced by perception.

[1] Cowell, Report on the Toles of Nuddea, 1867.
[2] See M. M., Appendix to Archbishop Thomson's Laws of Thought; also, Die Theorie des indischen Rationalisten von den Erkenntnismitteln, von R. Garbe, 1888.

by inference, by comparison, and by revealed authority.
Here we are brought back to the Pramanas again which
were discussed in the beginning, but among which one,
Anumana or inference, receives here a more special treatment. We are thus obliged, in following the Sutras, to
go over some of the ground again. Different systems of
philosophy differed, as we saw, in the number of Pramanas
which they admit, according to what each considers the
only trustworthy channels of knowledge.

Pramanas in different Philosophical Schools

One, Perception: Charvakas.
Two, Perception and inference: Vaiseshikas and
Buddhists.
Three, Perception, inference, and word (revelation) :
Sankhyas.
Four, Perception, inference, revelation, and comparison:
Naiyayikas.
Five, Perception, inference, revelation, comparison, and
presumption: Prabhakara (a Mimamsaka).
Six, Perception, inference, revelation, comparison, pre-
sumption, and not-being: Mimamsakas.
Others admit also Aitihya, tradition, Sambhava, equiva-
lence, Cheshta, gesture.

After sensuous knowledge, which takes cognisance of
substances, qualities, and actions, has been examined, the
question arises, how can we know things which are *not*
brought to us by the senses? How do we know, for
instance, that there is fire which we cannot see in a mountain, or that a mountain is a volcano, when all that we do
see is merely that the mountain smokes? We should
remember that there were three kinds of Anumana (Nyaya-
Sutras II, 37) called Purvavat, having the sign before, or
as the cause, Seshavat, having the sign after or as the
effect, and Samanyatordrishta, seen together. In the first
class the sign of past rain was the swelling of rivers; in
the second the sign of coming rain was the ants carrying
off their eggs; in the third the sign of the motion of the
sun was its being seen in different places. Knowledge of
things unseen, acquired in these three ways, is called in-

ferential knowledge (Anumana), and in order to arrive at it, we are told that we must be in possession of what is called a Vyapti. This, as we saw, was the most important word in an Indian syllogism. Literally it means pervasion. Vyapta means pervaded; Vyapya, what must be pervaded; Vyapaka, what pervades. This expression, to pervade, is used by logicians in the sense of invariable, inseparable or universal concomitance. Thus sea-water is always pervaded by saltness, it is inseparable from it, and in this sense Vyapya, what is to be pervaded, came to be used for what we should call the middle term in a syllogism. Vyapti, or invariable concomitance, may sometimes be taken as a general rule, or even as a general law, in some cases it is simply the *sine quo non.* It is such a Vyapti, for instance, that smoke is pervaded by or invariably connected with fire, or, as the Hindus say, that smokiness is pervaded by fieriness, not, however, fieriness by smokiness. We arrive by induction at the Vyapti that wherever there is smoke, there is fire, but not that wherever there is fire, there is smoke. The latter Vyapti in order to be true would require a condition or Upadhi, *viz.* that the firewood should be moist. If we once are in possession of a true Vyapti as smokiness being pervaded by fieriness, we only require what is called grouping or consideration (Paramarsa) in order to make the smoke, which we see rising from the mountain, a Paksha or member of our Vyapti, such as 'wherever there is smoke, there is fire.' The conclusion then follows that this mountain which shows smoke, must have fire.

All this may sound very clumsy to European logicians, but it would have been easy enough to translate it into our own more technical language. We might easily clothe Kanada in a Grecian garb and make him look almost like Aristotle. Instead of saying that inferential knowledge arises from discovering in an object something which is always pervaded by something else, and that the pervading predicate is predicable of all things of which the pervaded predicate is, we might have said that our knowledge that S is P arises from discovering that S is M, and M is P, or with Aristotle, *Ho sullogismos dia tou mesou to akron to trito deiknusin.* What Kanada calls one member of the pervasion, Paksha, *e.g.* the smoking mountain, might have been translated by subject or *terminus minor;* what pervades, Vyapaka or Sadhya, *e.g.* fieriness, by predicate or *terminus major;* and what is to be pervaded, Vyapya, *i.e.* smokiness, by *terminus medius.* But what should we have gained by this? All that is peculiar to Indian logic would have evaporated, and the remainder might have been taken for a clumsy imitation of Aristotle. *Multa fiunt eadem, sed aliter,* and it is this very thing, this *aliter,* that constitutes the principal charm of a comparative study of philosophy. Even such terms as syllogism or conclusion are inconvenient here, because they have with us an historical colouring and may throw a false light on the subject. The Sanskrit Anumana is not exactly the Greek *sumperasma,* but it means measuring something by means of something else. This is done by what we may call syllogism, but what the Hindus describe as Paramarsa or groping or trying to find in an object something which can be measured by something else or what can become the member of a pervasion. This corresponds in fact to the looking for a *terminus medius.* In Kapila's system (I, 61) the principal object of inference is said to be transcendent truth, that is, truth which transcends the horizon of our senses. Things which cannot be seen with our eyes, are known by inference, as fire is, when what is seen is smoke only. Gotama therefore defines the result of inference (I, 101) as knowledge of the connected, that is, as arising from the perception of a connection or a law. But, again, the relation of what pervades and what is pervaded is very different from what we should call the relative extension of two concepts. This will become more evident as we proceed. For the present we must remember that in the case before us the act of proving by means of Anumana consists in our knowing that there is in the mountain something always pervaded by, or inseparable-from something else, in our case, smoke always pervaded by fire, and that therefore the mountain, if it smokes, has fire.

By this process we arrive at Anumiti, the result of Anumana, or inferential knowledge, that the mountain is a volcano. So much for the inference for ourselves. Next follows the inference for others.

Anumana for Others

WHAT follows is taken from Annambhatta's Compendium. 'The act of concluding,' he says, 'is twofold, it being intended either for one's own benefit or for the benefit of others. The former is the means of arriving at knowledge for oneself, and the process is this. By repeated observation, as in the case of kitchen hearths and the like, we are reminded of a rule (Vyapti), such as that wherever we have seen smoke, we have seen fire. We now approach a mountain and wonder whether there may or may not be fire in it. We see the smoke, we remember the rule, and immediately perceive that the mountain itself is fiery. This is the process when we reason for ourselves.

But if we have to convince somebody else of what we, by inference, know to be true, the case is different. We then start with the assertion, The mountain is fiery. We are asked, Why? and we answer, Because it smokes. We then give our reason, or the major premiss, that all that smokes is fiery, as you may see, for instance, on a kitchen hearth and the like. Now you perceive that the mountain does smoke, and hence you will admit that I was right when I said that the mountain is fiery. This is called the five-membered form of exposition, and the five members are severally called,[1]—

(1) Assertion (Pratijna), the mountain has fire;

(2) Reason (Hetu[2]), because it has smoke;

(3) Instance (Udaharana or Nidarsana), look at the kitchen hearth, and remember the Vyapti between smoke and fire;

(4) Application (Upanaya), and the mountain has smoke;

(5) Conclusion (Nigamana), therefore it has fire[3].'

In both cases the process of inference is the same, but

---

[1] Nyaya-Sutras I, 32.

[2] Synonyms of Hetu are Apadesa, Limga, Pramana, and Karana. Vaiseshika-Sutras IX, 2, 4.

[3] The Vaiseshika terms are (1) Pratijna, (2) Apadesa, (3) Nidarsana, (4) Anusamdhana, (5) Pratyamnaya.

the second is supposed to be more rhetorical, more per-
suasive, and therefore more useful in controversy.

What is called by Annambhatta the conclusion for
oneself, corresponds *totidem verbis* to the first form of
Aristotle's syllogism:

> All that smokes is fiery,
> The mountain smokes;
> Therefore the mountain is fiery.

We must not forget, however, that whatever there is
of formal Logic in these short extracts, has but one object
with Gotama, that of describing knowledge as one of the
qualities of the Self, and as this knowledge is not confined
to sensuous perceptions, Gotama felt it incumbent on him
to explain the nature and prove the legitimacy of the inferential kind of knowledge also. It is not so much logic
as it is noetic that interested Kanada. He was clearly
aware of the inseparability of inductive and deductive
reasoning. The formal logician, from the time of Aristotle
to our own, takes a purely technical interest in the
machinery of the human mind, he collects, he arranges and
analyses the functions of our reasoning faculties, as they
fall under his observation. But the question which
occupies Gotama is, How it is that we know any thing
which we do not, nay which we cannot perceive by our
senses, in fact, how we can justify inferential knowledge.
From this point of view we can easily see that neither induction nor deduction, if taken by itself, would be sufficient
for him. Deductive reasoning may in itself be most useful
for forming Vyaptis, it may give a variety of different
aspects to our knowledge, but it can never add to it. And
if on one side Gotama cannot use deduction, because it
teaches nothing new, he cannot on the other rely entirely
on induction, because it cannot teach anything certain or
unconditional.

The only object of all knowledge, according to Gotama,
is absolute truth or Prama. He knew as well as Aristotle
that *epagoge* in order to prove the *holos* must be *diapanton*,
and that this is impossible. Knowledge gained by epagogic
reasoning is, strictly speaking, always *epi to polu*, and not
what Gotama would call Prama. The conclusion, f. i., at

which Aristotle arrives by way of induction, that animals with little bile are long-lived, might be called a Vyapti. He arrives at it by saying that man, horse, and mule (C) are long-lived (A); man, horse, and mule (C) have little bile (B); therefore all animals with little bile are long-lived. Gotama does not differ much from this, but he would express himself in a different way. He would say, wherever we see the attribute of little bile, we also see the attribute of long life, as for instance in men, horses, mules, &c. But there he would not stop. He would value this Vyapti merely as a means of establishing a new rule; he would use it as a means of deduction and say, 'Now we know that the elephant has little bile, therefore we know also that he is long-lived.' Or to use another instance, where Aristotle says that all men are mortal, Kanada would say that humanity is pervaded by mortality, or that we have never seen humanity without mortality; and where Aristotle concludes that kings are mortal because they belong to the class of men, Gotama, if he argued for himself only, and not for others, would say that kinghood is pervaded by manhood and manhood by mortality, and therefore kings are mortal.

It would be easy to bring objections against this kind of reasoning, and we shall see that Indian philosophers themselves have not been slow in bringing them forward, and likewise in answering them. One thing can be said in favour of the Indian method. If we go on accumulating instances to form an induction, if, as in the afore-mentioned case, we add horses, mules, men, and the like, we approximate no doubt more and more to a general rule, but we never eliminate all real, much less all possible, exceptions. The Hindu, on the contrary, by saying. 'Wherever we have seen the attribute of little bile, we have observed long life,' or better still, 'We have never observed long life without the attribute of little bile,' and by then giving a number of mere instances, and these by way of illustration only, excludes the reality, though not the possibility, of exceptions. He states, as a fact, that wherever the one has been, the other has been seen likewise, and thus throws the *onus probandi* as to any case to the contrary upon the other side. The Hindu knows the nature of induction

quite well enough to say in the very words of European
philosophers, that because in ninety-nine cases a Vyapti[1]
or rule has happened to be true, it does not follow that it
will be so in the hundredth case. If it can be proved, however, that there never has been an instance where smoke
was seen without fire, the mutual inherence and inseparable
connection of smoke and fire is more firmly established
than it would be by any number of accumulated actual
instances where the two have been seen together.

The conditions (Upadhis) under which it is allowable
to form a Vyapti, that is to say, to form a universal rule,
have greatly occupied the thoughts of Hindu philosophers.
Volumes after volumes have been written on the subject,
and though they may not throw any new light on the origin
of universals, they furnish at all events a curious parallel
to the endeavours of European philosophers in defence both
of inductive and deductive thinking.

It seems hardly time as yet to begin to criticise the inductive and the deductive methods as elaborated by Hindu
philosophers. We must first know them more fully. Such
objections as have hitherto been started were certainly not
unknown to Gotama and Kanada themselves. In accordance with their system of Purvapaksha and Uttarapaksha,
every conceivable objection was started by them and carefully analysed and answered. Thus it has been pointed
out by European philosophers that the proposition that
wherever there is smoke there is fire, would really lose its
universal character[2] by the introduction of the instance,
'as on the kitchen hearth.' But the Hindu logicians also
were perfectly aware of the fact that this instance is not
essential to a syllogism. They look upon the instance
simply as a helpful reminder for controversial purposes, as
an illustration to assist the memory, not as an essential
part of the process of the proof itself. It is meant to

---

[1] 'Satatah tahacharitayor api vyabhicharopalabdheh.' Anumana-
khanda of Tattvachintamani.

[2] Ritter, History of Philosophy, IV, p. 365, says that 'two members
of Kanada's argument are evidently superfluous, while, by the introduction of an example in the third, the universality of the conclusion
is vitiated.'

remind us that we must look out for a Vyapti between the smoke which we see, and the fire which is implied, but not seen. It is therefore in rhetorical syllogisms or syllogisms for others only that the instance has its proper place. In Sutra I, 35 Gotama says, 'The third member or example is some familiar case of the fact which, through its having a character which is· invariably attended by that which is to be established, establishes (in conjunction with the reason) the existence of that character which is to be established.' It is Indian rhetoric therefore far more than Indian logic that is responsible for the introduction of this third member which contains the objectionable instance; and rhetoric, though it is not logic, yet, as Whately says, is an offshoot of logic.

The fact is that Gotama cares far more for the formation of a Vyapti, pervasion, than for the manner in which it may serve hereafter as the basis of a syllogism, which must depend on the character of the Vyapti. A Vyapti was considered as threefold in the school of Gotama, as Anvaya-vyatireki, Kevalanvayi and Kevala-vyatireki. The first, the Anvaya-vyatireki, present and absent, is illustrated by such a case as, Where there is smoke, there is fire, and where fire is not, smoke is not. The second, or Kevalan-vayi, i.e. present only, is illustrated by such a case as, Whatever is cognisable is nameable, where it is impossible to bring forward anything that is not cognisable. The third case, or Kevala-vyatireki, is illustrated by a case such as, Earth is different from the other elements, because it is odorous. Here we could not go on and say, all that is different from the other elements has odour, because the only case in point (Udaharana) would again be earth. But we have to say, what is not different from the other elements is not odorous, as water (by itself). But this earth is not so, is not inodorous, and therefore it is not not-different from the other elements, but different from them, q.e.d.

Much attention has also been paid by Hindu philosophers to the working of the Upadhis or conditions assigned to a Vyapti. Thus in the ordinary Vyapti that there is smoke in a mountain, because there is fire, the presence of wet fuel was an Upadhi, or indispensable condition. This

Upadhi pervades what is to be established (Sadhya-vya-paka), in this case, fire, but it does not pervade what establishes (Sadhana-vyapaka), i.e. smoke, because fire is not pervaded by or invariably accompanied by wet fuel, as, for instance, in the case of a red-hot iron ball, where we have really fire without smoke. Hence it would not follow by necessity that there is fire because there is smoke, or that there is no fire because there is no smoke. How far the Indian mind may go in these minutiae of reasoning may be seen from the following instance given by Dr. Ballantyne in his Lectures on the Nyaya-philosophy, founded chiefly on the Tarkasamgraha, p. 59:

' To be the constant accompanier of what is to be established (Sadhya-vyapakatva) consists in the not being the counter-entity (Apratiyogitva) of any absolute non-existence (Atyantabhava) having the same subject of inhesion (Samanadhikarana) as that which is to be established. To be not the constant accompanier of the argument (Sadhanavyapakatva) consists in the being the counter-entity (Pratiyogitva) of some absolute non-existence [not impossibly] resident in that which possesses [the character tendered as an] argument.'

The credit of this translation belongs not to me, but to the late Dr. Ballantyne, who was assisted in unravelling these cobwebs of Nyaya logic by the Nyaya-Pandits of the Sanskrit College at Benares. Such Indian aid would seem to be almost indispensable for such an achievement.

CHAPTER IX

VAISESHIKA PHILOSOPHY

Date of Sutras

IT is fortunate that with regard to the Vaiseshika philosophy, or rather with regard to the Vaiseshika-Sutras, we are able to fix a date below which their composition cannot be placed. In the year 1885 Professor Leumann, well known by his valuable researches in Jaina literature, published an article, 'The old reports on the schisms of the Jainas,' in the *Indische Studien*, XVII, pp. 91-135. Among the various heresies there mentioned, the sixth, we are told, p. 121, was founded by the author of the Vaisesiya-sutta of the Chaulu race, and hence called Chauluga[1]. If there could be any doubt that this is meant for the Vaise-shika-Sutras it would at once be dispersed by the 144 so-called points of that system, as mentioned by the author, Jinabhadra. Jinabhadra's date is fixed by Professor Leumann in the eighth century A.D., and is certainly not later. This, it is true, is no great antiquity, still, if we consider the age of our Samkhya-Sutras, referred now to the thirteenth century A.D., even such a date, if only certain, would be worth having. But we can make another step backward. Haribhadra, originally a Brahman, but converted to Jainism, has left us a work called the Shaddar-sanasamuchchaya-sutram, which contains a short abstract of the six Darsanas in which the Vaiseshika-darsana is described as the sixth, and in that description likewise we meet with the most important technical terms of the Vaiseshika. This short but important text was published in the first volume of the *Giornale della Societa Asiatica Italiana*, 1887, and Sanskrit scholarship is greatly indebted to Professor C. Puini for this and other valuable contributions of his to Jaina literature. The author, Haribhadra, died in 1055 of the Vira-era, *i.e.* 585 Samvat, that is 528 A.D. This would give us an attestation for the Vaise-.

---

[1] Could this be meant for Auluka?

shika-Sutras as early as that of the Samkhya-karikas, if not earlier, and it is curious to observe that in Haribhadra's time the number six of the Darsanas was already firmly established. For, after describing the (1) Bauddha, (2) Naiyayika, (3) Samkhya, (4) Jaina, (5) Vaiseshika, and (6) Jaiminiya systems, he remarks, that if some consider the Vaiseshika not altogether different from the Nyaya, there would be only five orthodox systems (Astika), but that in that case the number six could be completed by the Lokayita (*sic*) system which he proceeds to describe, but which, of course, is not an Astika, but a most decided Nastika system of philosophy. It is curious to observe that here again the Vedanta-philosophy, and the Yoga also, are passed over in silence by the Jainas, though, for reasons explained before, we have no right to conclude from this that these systems had at that time not yet been reduced to a systematic form like the other four Darsanas. What we learn from this passage is that early in the sixth century A.D. the Nyaya, Samkhya, Vaiseshika, and Purva-Mimamsa systems of philosophy formed the subject of scientific study among the Jainas, and we may hope that a further search for Jaina MSS. may bring us some new discoveries, and some further light on the chronological development of philosophical studies in India.

Dates from Tibetan Sources

WHENEVER we shall know more of the sources from which Tibetan writers derived their information about Indian literary matters, more light may possibly come from thence on the dates of the Indian philosophical systems of thought also. It is true that the introduction of Buddhism into Tibet dates from the eighth century only, but the translators of Sanskrit originals, such as Santi Rakshita, Padma Sambhava, Dharmakirti, Dipamkara Srijnana and others, may have been in possession of much earlier information. In an account[1] of King Kanishka (85-106 A.D.) and his Great Council under Vasumitra and Purnaka, we read that there was at that time in Kashmir a Buddhist of the name of Sutra who maintained a large Buddhist congregation

[1] Journal of Buddhist Text Society, vol. I, p. 1 seq.

headed by a sage Dharmarakshita, and he is said to have belonged to the Vaiseshika school[1]. This would prove the existence of the Vaiseshika philosophy in the first century A.D., a date so welcome that we must not allow ourselves to accept it till we know what authority there was for the Tibetan writers to adopt it. It is taken from Sumpahi Choijung, and the same authority states that after the death of Kanishka, a rich householder of the name of Jati who lived at Asvaparanta in the north, invited Vasunetra, a monk of the Vaiseshika school, from Maru in the west, and another, Gosha Samgha from Bactria, and supported the native clergy, consisting of three hundred thousand monks, for a period of ten years.

Kanada

ALTHOUGH Nyaya and Vaiseshika have been often treated as sister philosophies, we must, after having examined Gotama's philosophy, give, for the sake of completeness, at least a general outline of Kanada's system also. It does not contain much that is peculiar to it, and seems to presuppose much that we found already in the other systems. Even the theory of Anus or atoms, generally cited as its peculiar character, was evidently known to the Nyaya, though it is more fully developed by the Vaiseshikas. It begins with the usual promise of teaching something from which springs elevation or the *summum bonum*, and that something Kanada calls Dharma or merit. From a particular kind of merit springs, according to Kanada, true knowledge of certain Padarthas, or categories, and from this once more the *summum bonum*. These categories, of which we spoke before as part of the Nyaya-philosophy, embrace the whole realm of knowledge, and are: (1) substance, Dravya; (2) quality, Guna; (3) action, Karman; (4) genus or community, Samanya, or what constitutes a genus; (5) species or particularity, Visesha, or what constitutes an individual; (6) inhesion or inseparability, Samavaya; (7) according to some, privation or negation, Abhava. These are to be considered by means of their mutual similarities and dissimilarities, that is, by showing how

---

[1] Ibid., vol. I, part 3, p. 19.

they differ and how far they agree. Here we have, indeed, what comes much nearer to Aristotle's categories than Gotama's Padarthas. These categories or predicaments were believed to contain an enumeration of all things capable of being named, i.e. of being known. If the number of Aristotle's categories was controverted, no wonder that those of Kanada should have met with the same fate. It has always been a moot point whether Abhava, non-existence, deserves a place among them, while some philosophers were anxious to add two more, namely, Sakti, potentia, and Sadrisya, similitude.

Substances

I. The substances, according to the Vaiseshikas, are: (1) earth, Prithivi; (2) water, Apah; (3) light, Tejas; (4) air, Vayu; (5) ether, Akasa; (6) time, Kala; (7) space, Dis; (8) self, Atman; (9) mind, Manas. These substances cannot exist without qualities, as little as qualities can exist without substances. The four at the head of the list are either eternal or non-eternal, and exist either in the form of atoms (Anus) or as material bodies. The non-eternal substances again exist as either inorganic, organic, or as organs of sense. The impulse given to the atoms comes from God, and in that restricted sense the Vaiseshika has to be accepted as theistic. God is Atman in its highest form. In its lower it is the individual soul. The former is one, and one only, the latter are innumerable.

Qualities

II. The principal qualities of these substances are: (1) colour, Rupa, in earth, water, and light; (2) taste, Rasa, in earth and water; (3) smell, Gandha, in earth; (4) touch, Sparsa, in earth, water, light, and air; (5) number, Samkhya, by which we perceive one or many; (6) extension or quantity, Parimana; (7) individuality or severalty, Prithaktva; (8) conjunction, Samyoga; (9) disjunction, Viyoga; (10) priority, Paratva; (11)[1] posteriority, Apa-

---

[1] Here follow in some lists as 11 to 15, gravity, fluidity, viscidity, and sound. The remaining Gunas are said to be perceptible by the mental organ only, not by the organs of sense.

ratva; (12) thought, Buddhi; (13-14) pleasure and pain, Sukha-duhkha; (15-16) desire and aversion, Ichchha-dveshau; (17)[1] will, effort, Prayatna.

Actions

III. The principal actions affecting the substances are: (1) throwing upwards, Utkshepana; (2) throwing down-wards, Avakshepana (or Apa); (3) contracting, Akunchana; (4) expanding, Utsarana (or Pras-); (5) going, Gamana. These actions or movements are sometimes identified with or traced back to the Samskaras, a word difficult to translate, and which has been rendered by dispositions and instincts, as applied to either animate or inanimate bodies. These Samskaras[2] have an important position both in the Samkhya- and in the Bauddha-philosophies. In the Tarkadipika Samskara is rendered even by Jati (jatih samskaratmika bhavati), i.e. nature or inborn peculiarity; and in the Tarkasamgraha it is represented as threefold (Vegah, Bhavana, and Sthitisthapakah).

In the Sutras which follow, Kanada tries to point out certain features which the three categories of substance, quality, and action share in common, and others which are peculiar to two, or to one only. In the course of this discussion he has frequently to dwell on the effects which they produce, and he therefore proceeds in the next lesson to examine the meaning of cause and effect, and likewise of genus, species, and individuals. It may be that the name of Vaiseshika was given to Kanada's philosophy from the differences, or Viseshas, which he establishes between sub-stances, qualities, and actions, or, it may be, from Visesha as a name of individual things, applicable therefore to atoms. But this, in the absence of decisive evidence, must for the present remain undetermined.

Cause

As to cause and effect, Kanada remarks that cause pre-cedes the effect, but that, in order to be a true cause, it

---

[1] Here again some authorities add Dharma, virtue, and Adharma, vice, Samskara, faculty or disposition, and Bhavana, imagination.

[2] See Garbe, Samkhya, p. 269 seq.

must be a constant antecedent, and the effect must be
unconditionally subsequent to it. There is an important
and often neglected difference between Karana and Kârana.
Karana, though it may mean cause, is properly the instrumental cause only, or simply the instrument. An axe, for
instance, is the Karana, or instrument, in felling a tree, but
it is not the Kârana, or cause. Causes, according to Kanada,
are threefold, intimate, non-intimate, and instrumental.
The threads, for instance, are the intimate cause of the
cloth, the sewing of the threads the non-intimate, and the
shuttle the instrumental cause.

Qualities Examined

In the second book Kanada examines the qualities of
earth, water, &c. He, like other philosophers, ascribes four
qualities to earth, three to water, two to light, one to air
(Akasa). These are the principal and characteristic qualities, but others are mentioned afterwards, making altogether fourteen for earth, such as colour, taste, smell, touch,
number, extension, individuality, conjunction, disjunction,
genus, species, gravity, fluidity, and permanence (II, 1, 31).
Qualities ascribed to Isvara, or the Lord, are number,
knowlelge, desire, and volition. In the case of air, which
is invisible, he uses touch as a proof of its existence, also
the rustling of leaves; and he does this in order to show
that air is not one only. Curiously enough Kanada, after
explaining that there is no visible mark of air (II, 1, 15)
but that its existence has to be proved by inference and by
revelation (II, 1, 17), takes the opportunity of proving, as
it were, by the way, the existence of God (II, 1, 18) by
saying that 'work and word are the signs of the substantial
existence of beings different from ourselves.' This, at least,
is what the commentators read in this Sutra, and they
include under beings different from ourselves, not only God,
but inspired sages also. It seems difficult to understand
how such things as earth and the name of earth could be
claimed as the work of the sages, but as far as God is
concerned, it seems certain that Kanada thinks he is able
to prove His existence, His omnipotence and omniscience
by two facts, that His name exists, and that His works.
exist, perceptible to the senses.

Immediately afterwards, Kanada proceeds to prove the existence of Akasa, ether, by showing that it must exist in order to account for the existence of sound, which is a quality, and as such requires the substratum of an eternal and special substance, as shown before. The question of sound is treated again more fully II, 2, 21-37.

A distinction is made afterwards between characteristic and adventitious qualities. If a garment, for instance, is perfumed by a flower, the smell is only an adventitious quality of the garment, while it is characteristic in the case of earth. Thus heat is characteristic of light, cold of water, &c.

Time

TIME, which was one of the eternal substances, is declared to manifest its existence by such marks as priority, posteriority, simultaneity, slowness, and quickness. The arguments in support of the substantiality of air and ether apply to time also, which is one, while its division into past, present, and future, hibernal, vernal, and autumnal, is due to extrinsic circumstances, such as the sun's revolutions. Time itself is one, eternal, and infinite.

Space

SPACE, again, is proved by our perceiving that one thing is remote from or near to another. Its oneness is proved as in the case of time; and its apparent diversity, such as east, south, west, and north, depends likewise on extrinsic circumstances only, such as the rising and setting of the sun. Like time it is one, eternal, and infinite.

So far Kanada has been chiefly occupied with external substances, their qualities and activities, and he now proceeds, according to the prescribed order, to consider the eighth substance, viz. Atman, the Self, the first in the list of his sixteen Padarthas. Like Gotama, Kanada also argues that the Atman must be different from the senses because while the senses apprehend each its own object only— (1) the sense of hearing, sound; (2) the sense of smelling, odour; (3) the sense of tasting, savour; (4) the sense of seeing, colour; (5) the sense of feeling, touch; it follows that there must be something else to apprehend them all, the work which in other philosophies was ascribed to Manas, at least in the first instance. Besides, the organs of sense are but instruments, and as such unconscious, and they require an agent who employs them. If we see a number of chariots skilfully driven, we know there must be a charioteer, and we know also that chariots and horses are different from the charioteer. The same applies to the senses of the body and to the Self, and shows that the senses by themselves could not perform the work that results in cognition. In defending this argument against all possible objections, Kanada, following the example of Gotama, is drawn away into a discussion of what is a valid and what is an invalid argument, and more particularly into an examination of what is a Vyapti, or an invariable concomitance, fit to serve as a true foundation for a syllogism.

Manas

But he soon leaves this subject, and, without finishing it, proceeds to a consideration of Manas, the ninth and last of the Dravyas or substances. This, too, is to him much the same that it was to Gotama, who treats it as the sixth of the Prameyas. In this place, as we saw, Manas might be translated by attention rather than by mind.

Anus or Atoms

What is thought to be peculiar to Kanada, nay the distinguishing feature of his philosophy, is the theory of Anus or atoms. They take the place of the Tanmatras in the Samkhya-philosophy. Though the idea of an atom is not unknown in the Nyaya-philosophy (Nyaya-Sutras IV, 2, 4-25), it is nowhere so fully worked out as in the Vaiseshika. Kanada argued that there must be somewhere a smallest thing, that excludes further analysis. Without this admission we should have a *regressus ad infinitum*, a most objectionable process in the eyes of all Indian philosophers. A mountain, he says, would not be larger than a mustard-seed. These smallest and invisible particles are held by Kanada to be eternal in themselves, but non-eternal as aggregates. As aggregates again they may be organised, organs, and inorganic. Thus the human body is earth organised, the power of smelling is the earthly organ, stones are inorganic.

It is, no doubt, very tempting to ascribe a Greek origin to Kanada's theory of atoms. But suppose that the atomic theory had really been borrowed from a Greek source, would it not be strange that Kanada's atoms are supposed never to assume visible dimensions till there is a combination of three double toms (Tryanuka), neither the simple nor the double atoms being supposed to be visible by themselves. I do not remember anything like this in Epicurean authors, and it seems to me to give quite an independent character to Kanada's view of the nature of an atom.

We are told that water, in its atomic state, is eternal, as an aggregate transient. Beings in the realm of Varuna (god of the sea) are organised, taste is the watery organ, rivers are water inorganic.

Light in its atomic state is eternal, as an aggregate transient. There are organic luminous bodies in the sun, sight or the visual ray is the luminous organ, burning fires are inorganic.

Air, again, is both atomic and an aggregate. Beings of the air, spirit, &c., are organised air; touch in the skin is the aerial organ, wind is inorganic air. Here it would seem as if we had something not very unlike the doctrine of Empedocles, *Gaie men gor gaiam opopamen, hudati d'hudor aitheri d'aithera diom atar puri pur oidelom.* But though we may discover the same thought in the philosophies of Kanada and Empedocles, the form which it takes in India is characteristically different from its Greek form.

Ether is always eternal and infinite. The sense of hearing is the ethereal organ: nay, it is supposed by some that ether is actually contained in the ear.

As to atoms, they are supposed to form first an aggregate of two, then an aggregate of three double atoms, then of four triple atoms, and so on. While single atoms are indestructible, composite atoms are by their very nature liable to decomposition, and, in that sense, to destruction. An atom, by itself invisible, is compared to the sixth part of a mote in a sunbeam.

Samanya

IV. As to Samanya, community, or, as we should say, genus, the fourth of Kanada's categories, it is supposed to be eternal, and a property common to several, and abiding in substance, in quality, and in action. It is distinguished by degrees, as high and low; the highest Samanya, or, as we should say, the highest genus (Jati) is Satta, mere being, afterwards differentiated by Upadhis, or limitations, and developed into ever so many subordinate species. The Buddhist philosophers naturally deny the existence of such a category, and maintain that all our experience has to do with single objects only.

Visesha

V. THESE single objects are what Kanada comprehends under his fifth category of Visesha, or that which constitutes the individuality or separateness of any object. This also is supposed to abide in eternal substances, so that it seems to have been conceived not as a mere abstraction, but as something real, that was there and could be discovered by means of analysis or abstraction.

Samavaya

VI. THE last category, with which we have met several times before, is one peculiar to Indian philosophy. Samavaya is translated by inhesion or inseparability. With Kanada also it is different from mere connection, Samyoga, such as obtains between horse and rider, or between milk and water mixed together. There is Samavaya between threads and cloth, between father and son, between two halves and a whole, between cause and effect, between substances and qualities, the two being interdependent and therefore inseparable.

Though this relationship is known in non-Indian philosophies, it has not received a name of its own, though such a term might have proved very useful in several

controversies. The relation between thought and word, for
instance, is not Samyoga, but Samavaya, inseparableness.

Abhava

VII. In addition to these six categories, some logicians
required a negative category also, that of Abhava or
absence. And this also they divided into different kinds.
into (1) Pragabhava, former not-being, applying to the
cloth before it was woven; (2) Dhvamsa, subsequent non-
being, as when a jar, being smashed, exists no longer as
a jar; and (3) Atyantabhava, absolute not-being, an impos·
sibility, such as the son of a barren woman; (4) Anyonya-
bhava, reciprocal negation, or mutual difference, such as we
see in the case of water and ice.

It may seem as if the Vaiseshika was rather a disjointed
and imperfect system. And to a certain extent it is so.
Though it presupposes a knowledge of the Nyaya-system,
it frequently goes over the same ground as the Nyaya,
though it does not quote *verbatim* from it. We should
hardly imagine that the Vaiseshika-Sutras would argue
against Upamana, or comparison, as a separate Pramana,
in addition to Pratyaksha (sense) and Anumana (inference),
unless in some other school it had been treated as an independent means of knowledge; and this school was, as we
saw, the Nyaya, which is so far shown to be anterior to
the Vaiseshika-philosophy. Kanada denies by no means
that comparison is a channel through which knowledge may
reach us, he only holds that it is not an independent channel,
but must be taken as a subdivision of another and larger
channel, viz., Anumana or inference. He probably held the
same opinion about Sabda, whether we take it in the sense
of the Veda or of an utterance of a recognised authority.
because the recognition of such an authority always implies.
as he rightly holds, a previous inference to support it. He
differs in this respect from the Charvaka secularist. who
denies the authority of the Veda outright, while Kanada
appeals to it in several places.

A similar case meets us in Gotama's Nyaya-Sutras (I, 16).
Here, apparently without any definite reason, Gotama tells
us in a separate aphorism that Buddhi (understanding),
Upalabdhi (apprehension), and Jnana (knowing) are not

different in meaning. Why should he say so, unless he had wanted to enter his protest against some one else who had taught that they meant different things? Now this some one else could only have been Kapila, who holds, as we saw, that Buddhi is a development of Prakriti or un-intelligent nature, and that conscious apprehension (Samvid) originates with the Purusha only. But here again, though Gotama seems to have had the tenets of the Samkhya-school in his eye, we have no right on this ground to say that our Samkhya-Sutras existed before the Nyaya-Sutras were composed. All we are justified in saying is that, like all the other systems of Indian philosophy, these two also emerged from a common stratum in which such opinions occupied the minds of various thinkers long before the final outcome settled down, and was labelled by such names as Samkhya, or Nyaya, Kapila, or Gotama, and long, of course, before the Samkhya-Sutras, which we now possess, were constructed.

The Six Systems

IT must have been observed how these six, or, if we include the Barhaspatya, these seven systems of philosophy, though they differ from each other and criticise each other, share nevertheless so many things in common that we can only understand them as products of one and the same soil, though cultivated by different hands. They all promise to teach the nature of the soul, and its relation to the God-head or to a Supreme Being. They all undertake to supply the means of knowing the nature of that Supreme Being, and through that knowledge to pave the way to supreme happiness. They all share the conviction that there is suffering in the world which is something irregular, has no right to exist, and should therefore be removed. Though there is a strong religious vein running through the six so-called orthodox systems, they belong to a phase of thought in which not only has the belief in the many Vedic gods long been superseded by a belief in a Supreme Deity, such as Prajapati, but this phase also has been left behind to make room for a faith in a Supreme Power, or in the Godhead which has no name but Brahman or Sat, ' I am what I am.' The Hindus themselves make indeed a distinction between the six orthodox systems. They have no word for orthodox; nay, we saw that some of these systems, though atheistic, were nevertheless treated as permissible doctrines, because they acknowledged the authority of the Veda. Orthodox might therefore be replaced by Vedic; and if atheism seems to us incompatible with Vedism or Vedic orthodoxy, we must remember that atheism with Indian philosophers means something very different from what it means with us. It means a denial of an active, busy, personal or humanised god only, who is called Isvara, the Lord. But behind him and above him Hindu philosophers recognised a Higher Power, whether they called it Brahman, or Paramatman, or Purusha. It was the denial of that reality which constituted a Nastika, a real heretic, one who could say of this invisible, yet omnipresent Being, Na asti, 'He is not.' Buddha, therefore, as well as Brihaspati, the Charvaka, was a Nastika, while both the Yoga and the Samkhya, the former Sesvara, with an Isvara, the other Anisvara, without an Isvara, the one theistic, the other atheistic, could be recognised as orthodox or Vedic.

The Hindus themselves were fully aware that some of their systems of philosophy differed from each other on essential points, and that some stood higher than others. Madhusudana clearly looked upon the Vedanta as the best of all philosophies, and so did Samkara, provided he was allowed to interpret the Sutras of Badarayana according to the principles of his own unyielding Monism. Madhusudana, as we saw, treated the Samkhya and Yoga by themselves as different from the two Mimamsas, Nyaya and Vaiseshika, and as belonging to Smriti rather than to Sruti. Vijnana-Bhikshu, a philosopher of considerable grasp, while fully recognising the difference between the six systems of philosophy, tried to discover a common truth behind them all, and to point out how they can be studied together, or rather in succession, and how all of them are meant to lead honest students into the way of truth.

In his Preface to the Samkhya-Sutras, so well edited and translated by Professor Garbe, Vijnana-Bhikshu says: " If we read in the Brihadaranyaka Upanishad II, 4, 5, and IV, 5, 6, that the Self must be seen, must be heard, must

be pondered and meditated on, hearing and the rest are
evidently pointed out as means of a direct vision of the
Self, by which the highest object of man can be realised.
If it is asked how these three things can be achieved,
Smriti or tradition answers: 'It must be heard from the
words of the Veda, it must be pondered on with proper
arguments, and, after that, it must be meditated on con-
tinuously. These are the means of the vision of the Self.'

'Meditated on,' that is, by means proposed in Yoga-
philosophy. Three things are known from passages of the
Veda. (1) the highest object of man, (2) knowledge
essential for its attainment, (3) the nature of the Atman
or Self which forms the object of such knowledge. And
it was the purpose of the Exalted. as manifested in the
form of Kapila, to teach, in his six-chaptered manual on
Viveka or distinction between Purusha and Prakriti, all the
arguments which are supported by Sruti.

If then it should be objected that we have already a
logical treatment of these subjects in the Nyaya and
Vaiseshika systems, rendering the Samkhya superfluous,
and that it is hardly possible that both—the Samkhya as
well as the Nyaya and Vaiseshika—could be means of right
knowledge, considering that each represents the Self in a
different form, the Nyaya and Vaiseshika as with qualities.
the Samkhya as without, thus clearly contradicting each
other, we answer No, by no means! Neither is the Samkhya
rendered superfluous by the Nyaya and Vaiseshika, nor do
they contradict each other. They differ from each other so
far only as Nyaya and Vaiseshika treat of the objects of
empirical knowledge, but the Samkhya of the highest truth.
The Nyaya and Vaiseshika, as they follow the common-
sense view that it is the Self that feels joy and pain, aim
at no more than at the first steps in knowledge, namely at
the recognition of the Atman as different from the body,
because it is impossible to enter *per saltum* into the most
abstruse wisdom. The knowledge of those preliminary
schools which is attained by simply removing the idea that
the Self is the body is no more than an empirical compre-
hension of facts, in the same manner as by a removal of
the misapprehension in taking a man at a distance for a
post, there follows the apprehension that he has hands, feet,

&c.. that is, a knowledge of the truth, yet purely empirical. If therefore we read the following verse from the Bhagavad-gita III, 29:

'Those who are deceived by the constituent Gunas of Prakriti, cling to the workings of the Gunas (Sattva, Rajas, and Tamas). Let therefore those who know the whole truth take care not to distract men of moderate understanding who do not as yet know the whole truth;'— we see that here the followers of the Nyaya and Vaiseshika systems, though they hold to the false belief that the Self can be an agent, are not treated as totally in error, but only as not knowing the whole truth, if compared with the Samkhyas, who know the whole truth. Even such knowledge as they possess, leads step by step by means of the lower impassiveness (Apara-vairagya) to liberation; while the knowledge of the Samkhyas only, as compared with the lower knowledge, is absolute knowledge, and leads by means of higher impassiveness (Paravairagya) straight to liberation. For it follows from the words quoted from the Bhagavad-gita that he only who knows that the Self is never an agent, can arrive at the whole truth, and from hundreds of true Vedic texts, such as Brih. Ar. Up. IV, 3, 22: 'Then he has overcome all the sorrows of the heart'; thinking that desires, &c., belong to the internal organ (Manas) only; or Brih. Ar. Up. IV, 3, 7: 'He, remaining the same (the Self), wanders through both worlds, as if thinking, and as if moving (but not really)'; or Brih. Ar. Up. IV, 3, 16: 'And whatever he may have seen there he is not followed (affected) by it'; and likewise from hundreds of similar passages in the Smriti, such as Bhag. III, 27: 'All works are performed by the constituents of matter (the Gunas of Prakriti); he only who is deceived by Ahamkara or subjectivation imagines that he is the agent'; and such as V. P. VI, 7, 22: 'The Self consists of bliss (Nirvana) and knowledge only, and is not contaminated (by the Gunas). The qualities (Gunas) are full of suffering, not of knowledge, and they belong to Prakriti, not to the Self'—from all such passages we say that it is clear that the knowledge proclaimed by Nyaya and Vaiseshika with regard to the highest subject is overcome.

By this, however, we do not mean to say that Nyaya

and Vaiseshika are not means of right knowledge, for their
teaching is not superseded by the Samkhya so far as
regards that portion which treats of the difference between
Self and the material body.   Here we must follow the
principle (laid down in the Purva-Mimamsa), that what
a word (chiefly) aims at, that is its meaning; (and apply it
to the systems of philosophy). The Nyaya simply repeats
the popular idea that joy pertains to the Self, without
referring to any further proofs; and this chapter therefore
is not to be considered as really essential (or as what the
Nyaya chiefly aims at).

But admitting that there is here no difference between
Nyaya-Vaiseshika and the Samkhya systems, is there not
a clear contradiction between the Samkhya on one side and
the Brahma-Mimamsa (Vedanta) and the Yoga on the
other? The former denies the existence of an eternal
Isvara, the two others maintain it.   Surely it cannot be
said that here also the contradiction between these systems,
the atheistic and theistic, can be removed by simply admitting, as before, two points of view, the metaphysical and
the empirical, as if the theistic doctrine existed only for the
sake of the worship of the multitude.   Such a decision
would here be impossible. The atheistic view that an Isvara
is difficult to know and therefore non-existent, may well
have been merely repeated by the Samkhyas, as a popular
idea, and in order to put an end to the desire of men for
acquiring a divine status and divine honours (by means of
penance, &c.), as in the case of the Naiyayikas when they
say that the Self possesses qualities (which must be taken
as merely a provisional remark).   In the Veda or elsewhere
Isvara, the anthropomorphic deity, is never explicitly denied,
so that one could say that theism should be taken as the
common popular view only.

In spite of all this we hold that here too these different
views are really due to empirical or to metaphysical con-
ceptions.

For as works like the Bhagavad-gita (XVI, 8) when
saying:
   ' Those say that the world is unreal, without support,
        without an Isvara.'
condemn the atheistic doctrine, we may very well suppose

that the Samkhyas simply repeated a common popular
view that there is no Isvara, in order to discourage the
striving after a divine status (so common among Saints).
or for some similar purpose. They would naturally think
that if they, so far following the materialists, did not deny
the existence of an active Isvara, the aequisition of the
discriminating knowledge (of the Samkhyas, between
Prakriti and Purusha) would be impeded, because those
who believe in an infinite, eternal and perfect Isvara, have
their thoughts entirely absorbed by this Isvara (so that
they might not attend to the essential doctrine of the
Samkhyas). No attack is made anywhere on theism, so
that the theistic doctrine of the Vedanta should be restricted
to sacrificial and similar purposes only. But from passages
like Mahabh. XII, 1167: ' No knowledge is equal to that
of the Samkhya, no power to that of the Yoga,' and again
XII, 11198: ' Let there be no doubt, the knowledge of the
Samkhya is considered the highest,' we should learn the
excellence of the Samkhya knowledge as superior to other
systems, though only with regard to that portion which
treats of the distinction of Self and Prakriti, and not with
regard to the portion that objects to an Isvara. Furthermore
from the consensus of Parasara also and all other eminent
authorities, we see that theism alone is absolutely true.
And from Parasara's Upa-purana and similar works the
truth of the Brahma-Mimamsa in its chapter on the Isvara
is perfectly manifest. There we read:

' In the systems of Akshapada and Kanada (Nyaya and
Vaiseshika), in the Samkhya and in the Yoga, whatever
portion is in conflict with the Veda, that has to be rejected
by all to whom the Veda is the only law.'

' In the systems of Jaimini and Vyasa (in the Purva and
Uttara-Mimamsa) there is nothing in conflict with the
Veda; for these two in their knowledge of the meaning of
the Veda have by means of the Veda fully mastered the
Veda.'

From other passages also the superior authority of the
Brahma-Mimamsa may be gathered, at least with regard
to that portion which treats of Isvara. Thus we read in
Mahabh. XII, 7663 seq.:

' Manifold philosophical doctrines have been propounded

by various teachers; but cling to that only which has been
settled by arguments, by the Veda, and by the practice of
good people.'

From this passage of the Mokshadharma also (XII, 7663),
and on account of the practice of Parasara and all eminent
authorities, it follows that the proof of the existence of an
Isvara, as proclaimed by the Brahma-Mimamsa, the Nyaya,
Vaiseshika and other systems, is to be accepted as the
strongest; and likewise because by passages in the Kurma
and other Puranas the ignorance of the Samkhyas with
regard to an Isvara has been clearly pronounced by Nara-
yana and others; e.g. 'Take thy refuge with the begin-
ningless and endless Brahman, whom the Samkhyas, though
strong as Yogins, are unable to perceive.'

Besides, that Isvara alone is the principal object of the
Brahma-Mimamsa is proved by the very first words and
by other indications. If then it had been refuted on
that principal point, the whole philosophy (the Brahma-
Mimamsa) would no longer be a means of right knowledge,
according to the principle, mentioned before, that what
a word chiefly aims at, that is its meaning. The chief aim
of the Samkhya, on the contrary, is not the denial of an
Isvara, but the highest object to be obtained by the Self
by means of the discrimination between body and Self
which leads to it. Hence, though it be superseded in that
part which treats of the denial of the Isvara, it will remain
as a means of right knowledge, and this once more according to the principle that what a word chiefly aims at, that
is its purport. The Samkhya has therefore its proper
sphere, and is vulnerable in that part only which treats of
the denial of the Isvara, the personal and active god.

Nor would it be right to say that in the Brahma-Mimamsa
Isvara may indeed be the principal object, but not its
eternal lordship or godhead. For, as the objection raised
in the Purvapaksha as to its (the Mimamsa's) allowing no
weight to the other Smritis cannot be sustained, it is clear
that Isvara can only be the object of the Brahma-Mimamsa,
provided he is characterised by eternal lordship.

If it is said that the first Sutra of the Brahma-Mimamsa
does not say ' Now then a wish to know the highest

Brahman,' and that therefore it does not by the word Brahman mean the Parabrahman, we must not on account of the Samkhya denial of an Isvara suppose that the Vedanta and Yoga systems likewise refer only to an evolved Isvara (a Karyesvara, a product of Prakriti), for in that case the whole string of Sutras from II, 2, 1, directed against the Samkhya and showing that mindless matter, being incapable of creating, cannot be established by mere reasoning, would be absurd; for if the God of the Vedanta were a made God, or a product of matter, the Samkhyas would have been right in teaching an independent matter (Prakriti). Lastly, the eternal character of Isvara is quite clear from such Yoga-Sutras as I, 26, 'He (God) is the Guru even of the oldest sages, because he is not limited by time,' and likewise from Vyasa's commentary on that Sutra. It is clear therefore that as the Samkhya means to deny the common popular anthropomorphic view of Isvara only, whether as a concession, or as a bold assertion, or, for some other reason, there exists no real contradiction between it, and the Brahma-Mimansa, and the Yoga.

Such concessions are found in other authoritative works also, as, for instance, in the Vishnu-Purana, I, 17, 83:

'O Daitya, these various opinions have I declared for those who admit a difference (who are not yet monists), by making a concession (to dualism). Let this abstract of mine be listened to.'

Nay it is possible that in some accredited systems also opinions should have been put forward in contradiction with the Veda in order to shut out bad men from a knowledge of the truth. Such parts would of course not be means of right knowledge, but the other and principal parts only, which are in harmony with Sruti and Smriti. Hence we see that in the Padma-Purana fault is found with all systems except the Brahma-Mimamsa and Yoga. Here, we see God (Siva) saying to Parvati:

'Listen, O goddess, I shall in succession tell you the heretical theories by the mere hearing of which even sages lose their knowledge.

'First of all, I myself have taught the Saiva, Pasupata and other systems, and afterwards others have been pro-

mulgated by Brahmans, who were filled by my powers.
Kanada has promulgated the great Vaiseshika doctrine,
Gautama the Nyaya, Kapila the Samkhya. The Brahman
Jaimini has composed a very large work of atheistic
character, the first of the two Mimamsas, which treat of
the meaning of the Veda.. Then, in order to destroy the
demons, Dhishana (Brihaspati) propounded the altogether
despicable Charvaka system; and Vishnu, under the disguise
of Buddha, propounded the erroneous Bauddha system
which teaches that people are to go naked, and should wear
blue or other coloured garments, while I myself, O goddess,
under the disguise of a Brahman (i.e. of Samkara) have
taught in this Kali age the doctrine of illusion (Maya)
which is false and only a disguised Buddhism. It is spread
far and wide in the world, and attributes a false meaning
to the words of the Veda. In it it is said that all works
should be relinquished, and after surrendering all works,
complete inactivity is recommended.

'I have taught in it the identity of the highest Self and
the individual Self, and have represented the highest form
of Brahman as entirely free from qualities; and this in
order to destroy the whole world in this Kali age. This
extensive, non-Vedic, deceptive doctrine has been propounded by me, as if it presented the true meaning of the
Veda, in order that all living things might perish.'

All this and more has been explained by me in the commentary on the Brahman-Mimamsa, and it is wrong therefore to say of any of the admittedly orthodox systems of
philosophy that it is not the means of right knowledge or
that it is refuted by others. For in reality none of them
is contradicted or refuted in what constitutes its own chief
object.

But, if it be asked whether the Samkhya-philosophy
has not likewise made a mere concession with regard to
the multiplicity of souls, we answer decidedly, No. For
on that point there is really no contradiction (between
the two, Samkhya and Vedanta) because it is shown in
the chapter which begins at Brahma-Sutras II, 3, 43, and
declares that the individual self is a part of the Highest
Self, because the multiplicity is stated (in the Veda); that
the Brahma-Mimamsa also recognises a multiplicity of

Atman. But that the individual souls, as conceived by the Samkhya, are Atman is certainly denied by the Vedanta, for it follows from Sutra IV, 1, 3: 'They know him and teach him as Atman,' that to the Vedantins, from the standpoint of absolute truth, the highest soul only is Atman. Nevertheless the Samkhya does not thereby lose its authoritative character, because it is not superseded by the Vedanta in what constitutes its own characteristic doctrine, namely that for the individual soul, the knowledge of its being different from everything else, constitutes the true means of liberation. There is no contradiction therefore, because the concepts of the manifold Atman and of the one Atman, so well known from Veda and tradition, can be fully reconciled according as we take an empirical or metaphysical view, as has been explained by ourselves in the *Commentary* on the' Brahma-Mimamsa—"*Sapienti sat.*"

I have given here this long extract from Vijnana-Bhikshu, though I have to confess that in several places the thread of the argument is difficult to follow, even after the care bestowed on disentangling it by Professor Garbe. Still, even as it is, it will be useful, I hope, as a good specimen of the Indian way of carrying on a philosophical controversy. Nay, in spite of all that has been said against Vijnana-Bhikshu, I cannot deny that to a certain extent he seems to me right in discerning a kind of unity behind the variety of the various philosophical systems, each being regarded as a step towards the highest and final truth. He certainly helps us to understand how it came to pass that the followers of systems which to our mind seem directly opposed to each other on very important points, managed to keep peace with each other and with the Veda, the highest authority in all matters religious, philosophical and moral. The idea that the largely accepted interpretation of the Vedanta-Sutras by Samkara was a perversion of the Veda and of Badarayana's Sutras, not much better than Buddhism, nay that Buddhism was the work of Vishnu, intended for the destruction of unbelievers, is very extraordinary, and evidently of late origin. Nay, nothing seems to me to show better that these Puranas, in the form in which we possess them, are of recent origin, and certainly

not the outcome of a period previous to the Renaissance of
Sanskrit literature, than passages like those quoted by
Vijnana-Bhikshu, representing the gods of the modern
Hindu pantheon as interfering with the ancient philosophy
of India, and propounding views which they know to be
erroneous with the intention of deceiving mankind.   Whatever the age of our philosophical Sutras may be, and some
of them, in the form in which we possess them, are certainly
more modern than our Puranas, yet the tradition or Param-
para which they represent must be much older; and in
trying to enter into the spirit of the Six Systems, we must
implicitly trust to their guidance, without allowing ourselves to be disturbed by the fancies of later sects.

INDEX

(The figure within parenthesis indicates the volume number)

www.ingramcontent.com/pod-product-compliance
Lightning Source LLC
Chambersburg PA
CBHW032013010726
47493CB00007B/2380